THE DAISY GAME

TAKE A CHANCE BOOK 7

NANCY WARREN

The Daisy Game, Take a Chance Book 7

Cover Design by Kim Killion

Copyright © 2018 by Nancy Warren

All rights reserved.

ISBN: ebook 978-1-928145-44-8

ISBN: print 978-1-928145-43-1

Ambleside Publishing

THE DAISY GAME

She's the most beautiful girl in town — and it sucks!

Lauren Chance is tired of getting hit on. Sick of having poetry written to her, songs composed to her eyes. She's a talented vet and all she wants is to heal animals.

But Joe Benbow is back. Joe, who had the worst crush of any guy back in high school, and made a prize fool of himself, embarrassing her into the bargain.

He's all grown up now. A firefighter in Hidden Falls to help his grandparents on the farm, and to scatter his father's ashes.

When Joe sees Lauren he can't believe she can still affect him. However, he's all grown up now and if there's one thing he knows how to do it's to act cool around women.

He's going to prove to Lauren that they can be friends.

But what if she wants something more?

The best way to keep up with new releases and special offers is to join Nancy's newsletter at NancyWarrenAuthor.com

CHAPTER 1

*W*hen Joe Benbow saw Lauren Chance for the first time in five years, she was elbow deep in a cow's rectum. And she was still the most beautiful woman he'd ever seen—or made a fool of himself over. As he headed toward them, he wasn't sure whose face looked less impressed by the proceedings, hers or the cow's.

His grandfather stood watching the examination. None of them had seen him yet, so he was able to watch at his leisure. He had time to feel something in his chest constrict. A hot mess of longing, desire, and humiliation: the remnants of a teenaged crush gone badly wrong.

Incredible that she should still affect him so strongly, nearly half a lifetime after he'd declared his teenaged love in a way that, at the time, he'd thought romantic, but that he now saw had been closer to deranged. His grand gesture hadn't even been original. He was pretty sure he'd gotten the idea from a movie. What had he been thinking?

Her hair, pulled up in a ponytail to keep it out of her face, was the color of a summer wheat field when the breeze blew through it. Not even the layers of bulky hoodie and flannel shirt over a faded T-shirt and old jeans could disguise the body that he and every boy in Hidden Falls, Oregon, used to dream about. But it was her face that compelled him. Eyes that blue ought to be due to fancy contact lenses, but hers weren't. Most girls with lips that plump and kissable would draw attention to them, but all he'd ever seen Lauren swipe on her lips was ChapStick. He doubted she even owned a cosmetic product. Irony was, she was more beautiful than any actress or model he'd ever seen in his life. Fourteen years had passed since he'd fallen so hard for her that summer, and in that time he'd moved away, seen the world, grown up, and dated loads of amazing women.

But seeing her again, he knew his instincts had been right. Lauren Chance really was the most beautiful girl in the world.

Her hunter green rain boots had sunk into ground that was more mud than land after recent rains had all but drowned Hidden Falls. Of all the things he missed about this place, the rain wasn't one of them.

Mostly what he missed was the man watching Lauren as she palpated the inside of one of the dairy herd—his grandpa, and maybe even more, his grandma.

Lauren reached even farther forward. Now most of her arm in its long rubber glove was inside the animal. He watched as her eyes closed, a sign she was concentrating. Good. He could look his fill at her, at the long, perfect neck, the curve of her jaw. Even her skin was flawless.

"What do you think?" his grandfather asked after a second or two. Ernest Benbow wasn't a patient man.

Lauren's eyes opened and she nodded. "I can feel liquid when I palpate the uterus, and there's something in there." She took another moment, nodded again. "Yep, there's something in there, all right. Maybe *two* somethings." She withdrew her arm and patted the cow's rump as though thanking the animal for being a good sport, before turning to Ernest. "Congratulations. I'd say she's about three months along. Probably with twins."

"Good, good." His grandparents had been dairy farmers in Hidden Falls for half a century and it was here on the farm that Joe had spent every summer after his parents split up. Grandma and Grandpa had given him a place to stay, all the good home cooking he could eat, stability, values. In exchange, he'd worked his butt off. Rising way too early for chores and learning young that farming was a round-the-clock enterprise.

He walked forward now, his feet squelching through the mud. "Morning."

His grandfather looked up and his weathered face cracked into a smile, "Joe! Wasn't expecting you 'til tomorrow." He extended his hand, old style. Ernest had never been one for hugging. He was a handshake or backslap man all the way.

Joe turned to Lauren, who took an involuntary step back as though worried he'd push a sonnet into her hand, or drop to his knees in the mud and beg her to be his. It seemed she hadn't forgotten his awful crush any more than he had. As though to cover her instinctive withdrawal, she laughed and said, "I'd shake your hand, too, but—"

He chuckled obediently and tried not to feel like a teenaged fool. How was it she still made him feel like one? He'd been back to see his grandparents since he'd last seen her, before she headed to college, but on every one of his visits since, she'd been away at vet school or working on a practicum far away. And now she was back.

"I heard you're a DVM now," he said. "Congratulations."

She stripped off the gloves with the ease of practice. "Thanks. I was lucky to get taken on by the best veterinary clinic in the area."

"They taught her well," Ernest said. "And she's got a way with animals. They're easy with her."

"They always were," he said, remembering how she'd always been nursing some creature back to health when she was younger. A rabbit with a torn ear, a crow with a broken wing.

When his grandparents' border collie bitch had a pup that wasn't thriving, they hadn't called in the expensive vet, they'd asked Lauren to take a look at it. Well, he had. Ernest was old school and inclined to think that a runt that couldn't nurse wasn't much use. "Let nature take its course," he'd said, but Joe had held the tiny pup, no bigger than his hand, and experienced the urge to rescue and protect. The same urge that had led to his current career as a firefighter.

Lauren Chance was already known as a girl who had a natural ability with animals. He'd phoned her on the sly and, following her instructions, had bundled the tiny thing into a box with old blankets and a hot water bottle. Then he'd borrowed Grandma's car and driven the tiny pup out to the Chance place.

He didn't know until later that Lauren had slept with the dog in her room and got up every two hours all through the night to feed it. The dog had a white patch of fur around his right eye, so they called him Patch. When he was a little stronger, they'd been able to return the dog to its mother.

After the pups were weaned, and his grandfather had told him he could choose one of the litter for his own, he'd chosen Patch.

"But he's the runt," Ernest had protested.

"He's got attitude. Fought for his life and won." Also hopelessly in love with Lauren. "I respect that."

And so Patch was his. Still was. As though her thoughts had run on the same lines, Lauren asked, "How's Patch?"

"Visiting with Grandma. I thought I'd leave him with her for a bit."

Ernest made a sound like sandpaper over metal. "Useless dog's scared of cows. Bet he wouldn't come out."

"They can't all be herders," he said mildly, wondering why he felt the need to defend his dog. "And he's a great pet."

"I'd love to see him," Lauren said before Ernest could give his usual lecture about working dogs versus lapdogs.

"You know he'd love to see you. I have to warn you, though, he's definitely slowing down."

"Well, he must be fifteen. Of course he's slowing down."

"Come up to the house for coffee," Ernest said. "Velma baked you an apple cake."

She smiled her delight at that and he had the opportunity to see that yes, her teeth were still that perfect gleaming white that had nothing to do with chemical strips. It was as though God had said, *For fun, I'm going to make a perfect beauty*, and created Lauren.

"She doesn't have to do that."

"She likes to do it. You'll never stop that woman from baking," Ernest said with undisguised pride. Everybody in the county knew Velma's apple cake. Even Iris, Lauren's sister who owned the best bakery for miles, couldn't make one half as good, and Velma was never going to part with the recipe.

"I'll pack up here and then come up to the house."

Ernest picked up the leading rope and headed back toward the fenced field with the pregnant cow in tow. "Go on up to the house, son, and tell your grandma to get the coffee on."

He'd have liked to stay with Lauren and catch up on old times, but he imagined a vet's schedule was tight and Ernest was a man who valued efficiency. He'd let Velma know the vet was on her way and the coffee would be freshly brewed when she got there.

He stuck to the gravel road as he walked back toward the house, his sneakers now caked in mud. They'd been comfortable for driving in, but he should have remembered to change into boots before heading out onto the farmland. Truth was, he'd been too eager to see Lauren.

As he strode back up to the house he wondered how he'd made it to thirty without getting over the summertime crush he'd been nursing now for half his lifetime.

Even her voice thrilled him, as he heard her call out to Ernest that she'd be back in a week to check on the three pregnant cows.

He took off his shoes in the mudroom and Patch came trotting up to welcome him, since they'd been separated for all of about seven minutes. When he walked into the big family kitchen, the smell of fresh-baked apple cake walloped him with the feeling of home. Velma wore her white hair short, and was dressed in comfortable black slacks and a purple zip-up hoodie with a flower embroidered on the front of it. Her face showed her age with its wrinkled skin and a few age spots, but her eyes glowed with life. She was grandmother, mother, and friend rolled into one and he loved her more than anyone in the world. His father was both their family link and their shared tragedy.

"Grandpa said to get the coffee on. Vet's on her way." They both glanced toward the coffee machine and he saw the fresh coffee already dripping into the carafe.

She cut up the cake efficiently and put the squares on one of her blue and white china plates. Cloth napkins and serving plates were already on the round oak table, where they ate every meal but Sunday dinner unless they were entertaining. A second cake was wrapped, all ready for Lauren to take away with her.

If he'd known Lauren would be here, Joe didn't think he would have returned to Hidden Falls. He could've tipped his dad into the waters off Bali, or scattered his ashes outside one of his favorite dive bars. He doubted his dad would've cared. He'd brought his ashes home for Ernest and Velma, he supposed, so that finally they could have their son home on the farm that meant so much to them.

How had Grandma never told him that Lauren had moved back to Hidden Falls? They emailed regularly and spoke on the phone at least once a week. That she was a vet made perfect sense. She'd always preferred animals to people, but why hadn't Grandma told him that she'd moved home to practice?

There ought to be a statute of limitations on humiliation, but he discovered there wasn't. He felt as smitten when he saw her now as he had as a besotted teen. Did it help that he wasn't the only guy who'd ever tripped over his own tongue when Lauren was around? There was something about her that made a man love-crazed. Even with a long line of men, young and old, vying for the title of biggest fool where Lauren Chance was concerned, he had a sneaking suspicion his name might top the list.

He'd written her *poetry*. He squirmed inside. He'd never composed a verse in his life—barely read one—and yet, at sixteen, when he'd gone from thinking she was a cool girl to falling in love with her, he'd thought writing her a poem would be a good plan.

It was as though obsession had crawled into his skull and ripped away his brain and then pumped his heart up to about fifteen times its normal size until he was nothing but a brainless, oversized heart, like a cartoon you'd see on Valentine's Day. He remembered rhyming *heart* with *dart* and *love* with *that of* and thankfully he couldn't remember any more. With luck she'd burned his only effort at poetry, along with all the other foolish poems and pictures and songs and carved animals she'd received. Not all from him, thank God.

Maybe he still would've been okay if he hadn't decided one night to serenade her at her window. He'd been a lonely kid, his mom long gone on a motorcycle with a guy whose name he never did learn. She said she'd call and, of course, she never did.

7

The fact that his dad was the most stable of the two still made him shake his head.

If he hadn't had Grandma and Grandpa, he didn't know what would have happened to him. For sure, he wouldn't have fallen for Lauren and poured all the love he was capable of into trying to win her. If he ever met John Cusack, or better yet, Cameron Crowe, he was going to give them a piece of his mind. When he'd watched *Say Anything...* as a cable rerun, it was as though he'd received personal instructions on how to win the girl of his dreams.

He wasn't going to hold a boombox over his head. That seemed lame. He'd go one better. He'd learned a few chords on the guitar, written his first and, thankfully, only love song and then, young jackass that he was, sung it under her window.

How had he not remembered that the Chance house was full of people, nearly half of them teenaged boys? While he'd poured out his heart in a song that included lyrics like, *Baby, all I want is you,* the Chance boys had taken exquisite enjoyment in howling out the window shouting abuse. In his fantasies, Lauren would come out of the house, wearing something white and flowing, but short enough to reveal her excellent legs. She'd walk up to him and let him know she was his forever.

The reality was so very different.

He'd heard Lauren beg her brothers to leave him alone. And not because she was enjoying his song, he could tell even then. Her face was red with embarrassment as she'd put her head out of the window and thanked him for his song. And suggested he should get on home.

He hadn't listened. He had more verses to sing! Still howling with glee, the Chance brothers had withdrawn their heads into their various windows and the house had quieted. He tried for a *Romeo and Juliet* moment. He wanted to climb up to her bedroom window, find her leaning out, her eyes lit with moonlight, but the Chance family home was a squat rambler and when she leaned out the window she begged him, with tears in her eyes, to please just go home.

He soon discovered why. The Chance boys suddenly surrounded him and he was hoisted up bodily and carried away from the house. He heard Lauren calling, "Don't hurt him. Please don't hurt him."

If he'd been able to fight all six of them and been beaten to a pulp by the unfair odds, at least he'd have been a romantic figure.

They hadn't even left him that much dignity. After carrying him like a squirming barnyard animal across a field and past a barn, he heard Evan—at least, he thought it was Evan—call, "One, two, three!" and then he was sailing through the air. With a splash and a shock of cold water, he found himself thrashing around in a pond.

That was the moment he stopped being a boy.

That was the first year since he'd been coming to his grandparents' home that he left before the summer was over.

That was the year he caught the Greyhound back to his dad's cheap rental before he was expected.

He knew that physical distance was the only way he could stop torturing himself over a pretty young girl who wanted nothing to do with him. And he'd managed always to keep his distance. They'd seen each other over the years, but never close enough to have a conversation. Until today.

It hadn't occurred to him that she'd return to Hidden Falls. He'd imagined her in some thriving city somewhere, as beautiful and unattainable as ever, and also far away. So to see her here was almost too much. If it weren't for the burden of worrying about his grandparents and the fact that he had to do something with his dad's ashes, he'd have left that afternoon. Because he'd seen the flash of discomfort in her eyes when she saw him. She was worried he was going to embarrass her again and, heaven help him, she might be right. She could wear flannel shirts and dumpy jeans and abstain from makeup, but nothing could hide her beauty.

There was also something about her that had nothing to do with her physical beauty. Something that still called to him.

If he spent much time around Lauren Chance, he was going to be as bad a goner as he had been at sixteen. A teenager who didn't know much about girls had some excuse. A grown man with years of experience under his belt had none.

His grandpa had never known anything of the foolishness going on under his roof, of course, but Grandma had. When he'd come home that night with his clothes soaked and his heart broken, she'd given him some advice that he'd never forgotten. She'd hustled him into a hot shower, and while he was warming up, prepared hot chocolate. Then she sat him down at the kitchen table and said, "The right girl's out there. And you'll know it's right when she looks at you and her eyes light up. You won't have to say anything. You won't have to write poetry or songs or impress her with feats of daring or heroism. She'll look into your eyes and you'll look into hers and you'll know."

At that moment, when his heart was raw and scraped and shattered and hurting, he hadn't wanted to believe there'd ever be anyone for him but Lauren. "But she's the only one I want," he all but shouted.

She'd shook her head, her eyes full of sympathy. "You can't make another person love you. The more you try to pull them toward you, the more you push them away."

"Was it like that for you and Grandpa? You just knew?"

She'd nodded, slowly, and her face grew soft. "If you could've seen your grandfather in his prime." She seemed to be looking back into the past and he could've sworn her face grew more girlish. "All the girls were after him. He was so tall and handsome, like one of the movie stars in westerns. Times weren't easy around here, but he was a hard worker. And then he'd get himself cleaned up and go into town for the dances on Saturday night. He always asked me to dance, but I wasn't the only one. There were probably half a dozen of us single girls that he'd dance with in an evening. And, of course, we were doing the same, dancing with all the single boys.

"I suppose it was our version of that online dating you do today. He'd dance with one girl, then another. I'd do the same with the young men. We were working out which one we liked. And then one day he dropped by my parents' house and asked if I'd like to go for a ride. He had this old car that he was so proud of. I did, of course, and he brought me here, and showed me the land he was hoping to buy. He used to come here and daydream. And the way he'd look at me—I think I knew he was in love with me before he did."

His young heart had ached. "You make it sound so easy."

She'd reached out and put her hand over his. "And it is. When you're with the right person, it is easy, because you fit together and you know it's right. I'm not saying there won't be arguments or tough times. Lord knows, Ernest and me, we've had years when we weren't sure we could keep the farm, we had a son who didn't want to be a dairy farmer." She'd not said another word about his dad, but it was pretty obvious his old man wasn't a son anyone would be proud of. "We were never able to have more children. But now we get to spend the summers with you, so that's a blessing we didn't see coming. It hasn't been easy. Life never is. But it's been right. With me and Ernest, it's just been right. And it will be for you, too. Be patient."

He'd been sixteen. He had no idea how to be patient. He only knew one thing. "I can't stay here."

She had nodded. "I know."

She'd smoothed things over with Ernest, but he knew he had

let them down, not being there right to the end of the summer to help with the haying and all the rest of the chores.

First love. He shook his head at his own youthful insanity. He'd never felt anything that strong or visceral in all the years and all the women since. He doubted he ever would.

"So, Lauren's back for good," his grandmother said, almost as though she'd been following his thoughts.

"So I see."

Grandma bustled around, already planning dinner. "Such a pretty girl. You'd think she'd be married by now. But seems like she's married to her job."

He only hoped he hadn't put Lauren off men forever. "She seems like a good vet," Joe said, keeping his tone neutral.

"Ernest says she's the best we've ever had. And you know how difficult he is to please."

Patch stood behind her, obviously hoping for a treat. "You spoil that dog." She sounded stern, but he knew Patch wouldn't hang around her if she wasn't a soft touch.

"How are you making out with your father's affairs?" she asked as she walked the plate of cake over to the table.

Affairs. There'd been plenty of those over the years, but he knew his grandmother referred to the practical affairs of death. Frank Benbow had failed at marriage, fatherhood, and business. He'd spent the last few years of his life in Bali, where he called himself a digital entrepreneur, but from what Joe had been able to discover, his definition of *digital entrepreneur* was hanging around in bars surfing the Net.

When he died, aged fifty-eight, of a heart attack, Joe's first reaction had been anger. He'd believed, deep down, that they'd have time to sort out their differences, to have some kind of relationship that didn't involve him wiring his dad money "just to tide me over until my app launches."

When he'd flown over to clean up Frank's affairs, he'd

discovered three women who thought they had claims on his estate. Of course, the estate, like the app, was a figment of his dad's imagination. He'd had the body cremated and, instead of a service, held a wake at Frank's favorite bar. As the beer and stories flowed, he had the sense of his dad in his last years as a likeable loser.

That was pretty much the way he thought of him, too.

He paid the tab at the end of the night, packed up the box of cremated remains, paid the outstanding rent on the beach shack where Dad had been living, and disposed of his possessions. The saddest thing was, there wasn't one thing left he'd have wanted to remember his dad by. He'd sold his watch and signet ring long ago. His ancient computer was missing—probably stolen—and his dad had never been one for old family photos. Maybe they made him feel guilty. Or old. So, he'd given away or tossed clothes and cooking items and junk, and flown back.

What was left of his dad was currently sitting in the back of his SUV. He hadn't known where to scatter the ashes and decided to bring them home, to Hidden Falls.

"I got it done," he said in answer to his grandmother's question, without elaborating.

He didn't need to. Grandma wasn't blind to her son's faults. She said, "If you need some money to cover things, your grandfather and I can help." He knew how hard they worked to hang on to the land and business, and how they needed to be thrifty to stay afloat. He shook his head and did something he almost never did with his grandparents.

He lied. "He had enough money left to cover his final expenses."

The glance she sent him told him she knew he'd lied, and that she understood why he had. She simply nodded. "Well, if you change your mind, we always keep a little extra put by for a rainy day."

And with the number of rainy days they got in the Pacific Northwest, they needed it.

Then she turned to Joe and said, "We're so glad you had your father's service in Bali. In a way, it would have been nice to bury him here in Hidden Falls, or scatter his ashes on our property." She sighed, sadly. "But then we wouldn't ever have been able to sell this place. Ernest and me, we went to church and said our good-byes in our own way. And you celebrated your dad's life in the place he chose to end his days. Now we can all move on."

For a stunned moment he simply stared at her. Of course, he'd kept her up to date on the details, and he must have mentioned the wake in Bali, but he supposed he'd never specifically told them he was bringing Dad's ashes home. How could he tell her now? When she and Ernest had already done their grieving?

Once more, it seemed, Frank was going to be a problem.

"How long can you stay?"

He'd taken a compassionate leave from the fire department, as well as his vacation, but he couldn't stay away indefinitely. "A few weeks."

She beamed at him. "Wonderful."

Yeah, wonderful. And now what was he going to do with his dad?

CHAPTER 2

$\mathcal{L}$ auren sat in her truck filling out her paperwork. She travelled with a tablet computer, but her hands got so messy that she preferred to keep manual records out in the field and fill in on the computer later. Besides, Ernest still preferred paper receipts. He was old school and she didn't think he had any intention of graduating.

Ernest and Velma had a good, healthy herd. They weren't the kind to cut corners; they were the kind of people she loved to work with. They took pride in their animals, in the milk and cheese that were part of a local cooperative, but they were aging and the years of toil showed in the deep lines carved in Ernest's rugged face. Too much work, early mornings, changes in the price of milk, diseases that could wipe out a herd—those were the burdens carried by the small dairy farmer.

Not today, though.

These cows were healthy and strong. She hoped, for Velma and Ernest's sake, they would stay that way. She'd do everything she could to help. But what would happen when Ernest and Velma were too old to continue? Not many young people wanted to farm anymore.

Having finished her paperwork, she headed up to the house, knowing she'd put off going in as long as she could.

Because Joe was back.

He'd changed a lot since she'd last seen him. He'd filled out, grown into the rugged handsomeness that was still evident in his grandfather. She knew he was a firefighter and something of the toughness of his profession came through in his manner— even the way he stood, solid and capable. But when she'd looked into his eyes, she still saw the eyes of that boy who had obsessed over her until the memorable and unfortunate incident of the midnight serenade. Had he not remembered that she lived with six brothers? They'd made short work of her youthful troubadour and, naturally, she'd been the butt of the family jokes for weeks afterward.

Even after all these years, she recognized the expression in his eyes. Damn! He wasn't obnoxious the way some guys were, but she felt his attraction the way she sensed warmth in a room, or the scent of rain in the air. She was so tired of this! She longed to be old and past being desirable to the other sex the way some people longed to reverse the aging process.

Well, he was only visiting, and she'd be careful not to encourage him. Clear boundaries, she reminded herself. All she needed to do was be clear about her own boundaries.

She walked into the farmhouse without knocking, toed off her filthy boots, shucked her hoodie, and inspected her old jeans. There was nothing too disgusting on them, and Velma was an experienced farm wife. She'd put a towel down over the chair before letting Ernest or Lauren sit.

Patch must have heard the door, for the dog came running in, tail wagging, and began sniffing her jeans as though they were a buffet table. She loved all animals, but she had a special kinship with this one. Of course, he was old now, and there was more gray in his muzzle than there had been the last time she saw him, and the eyes that gazed at her adoringly were clouded, but as she patted him she reassured them both. "You look pretty good for an old dude." He wagged his tail some more at that and followed her as she washed up in the powder room adjacent to the mud room. Patch herded her into the kitchen.

Velma greeted her with a hug, then stood back a step. "Look at you. You get prettier every day."

She felt herself stiffen and tried to prevent the response from showing. Ernest opened his mouth and she could no more have forestalled the next words than she could have changed the course of the sun in the sky. "When are you going to settle on one of the young men who are all crazy about you?" He looked to Joe, already sitting at the table. "The way they make fools of themselves over this pretty girl would make you laugh."

Joe didn't look as though he wanted to laugh. Ernest must never have learned about his grandson's famous serenade. Which made him one of a small minority of Hidden Falls residents.

"Coffee smells great," she said, by way of a hint to change the subject.

It worked. "You sit down and I'll pour you a cup," Velma said. "And I've got an apple cake for you to take home."

"It's the only reason I come here," she teased. "It's not about your herd at all." There were two seats at the table with towels already covering the upholstery. She sat on an old towel with faded pink roses that had frayed down one side.

"Oh, now you're being silly," Velma said, looking pleased all the same.

"Iris will be over to try a piece of this cake the minute I get home. She can't figure out if it's the species of apple, or the combination of spices, or if there's some secret ingredient in the streusel. It's fun to watch her eat a piece of your apple cake like it's a science experiment."

Ernest took his seat beside her, on an old navy blue towel with a bleach stain in the middle. "You could torture Velma and she'd never give away her secret recipe," he said, pouring a liberal dose of cream into his coffee. "And tell Iris there's no point breaking into the house and snooping, because Velma's never written it down." He was as proud of his wife as a man married for more than fifty years could be. It always made her happy to be around them. They reminded her of her parents. But her quiet pleasure was dimmed by a kind of haunting sadness. Would she ever find a man who would love the woman she was and not some fantasy he'd made up around her looks?

Iris was another one who seemed well on her way to a life of bliss; happily married and with her family well begun. "Speaking of Iris, how are the twins?" Velma asked.

"Too much of a handful for you to worry about Iris breaking into your house. She barely has time to shower. But they are perfect." She was pulling out her phone to show off the latest photos of her niece and nephew when Joe said, "Iris had twins?"

Ernest shook his head at his grandson. "You don't spend enough time around here, Joe." It was said mildly, but she knew how much they loved their grandson and how much they missed him. Ernest made no secret of the fact that he'd hoped Joe would one day take over his farm.

"Joe's busy keeping the people of San Diego safe. Being a firefighter is a very important job," Velma said. Of course, she'd have defended Joe no matter why he rejected farming. Next to Ernest, Joe was the love of her life.

"I'll be here for a few weeks, Grandpa. You can work me as hard as you want, and maybe we can look into hiring some help."

Ernest nodded, but there was sadness in the lines of his face. They all knew deep down that without someone in the next generation taking over, Ernest and Velma would have to sell the farm they'd spent their whole lives building. Joe shifted uncomfortably on his chair.

To break the atmosphere, she passed Velma her phone. "Here are the twins. This was taken last week at Mom's Sunday dinner."

"Oh, aren't they precious. And they grow so fast."

"Yep. They're nine months old and crawling all over the place. It pretty much takes our whole extended family to keep track of them."

She passed the phone to Joe, who said, "Cute kids," and passed it back.

Velma sighed. "Time goes so quickly. And in some ways so slowly. It seems only yesterday your father was that small. And then it was you. And soon you'll have your own little ones." Her eyes lit up. "I can't wait to be a great-grandmother. What are you now, thirty? It's time you got going."

Lauren had to stifle a snicker at the look on Joe's face. He looked well and truly trapped. Ernest said, "Now, Velma, you leave the boy be. He'll get to fathering when he's ready."

"How long does he need?"

Joe looked at Lauren and shook his head. "Sitting right here, Grandma and Grandpa."

"What about that nice girlfriend?" Velma wanted to know. "Kelly, isn't that her name? The nurse?"

"She's a paramedic. Nothing happened." He shrugged. "We both moved on."

"Never mind," she said soothingly, "There are plenty of fish in the sea."

"Thanks, Grandma."

Patch came up and put his head in Joe's lap, as though he felt his owner's discomfort at the embarrassing questions. At least, knowing he'd recently had a girlfriend calmed her a little. What —did she think that Joe had never looked at another woman in fourteen years? Still, hearing about other women in his life was comforting.

And she could see why he'd draw female attention. He'd grown into a very nice-looking guy. He looked like Ernest had as a young man. Velma had shown her pictures and they both agreed he'd been a dead ringer for the young Clint Eastwood. Joe had something of the same look, long and lanky, with the kind of face that looked as though it should be squinting down the barrel of a shotgun. Wearing a cowboy hat, boots, and spurs. He wore his brown hair short now and a glance at his body suggested he'd spent a lot of the time since she'd last seen him working out. The guy was buff.

She checked the time on her phone, finished her coffee, and rose. "Thanks for the coffee and cake, Velma. I've got to get to my next appointment."

Velma got to her feet and retrieved the second cake. "It was nice to see you."

"It was nice to see you, too. I'm going to enjoy every bite of this cake."

"I'll walk you out," Joe said, getting to his feet.

She was immediately uncomfortable. What if he asked her out? Again? She hated hurting people's feelings, wished they wouldn't put her in the position of having to do it. She hugged the cake tightly to her chest, like an apple- and cinnamon-scented shield. "It's okay."

"I want to talk to you."

Well, not much she could say to that. Except she'd make it clear she was in a hurry to get to her next job.

Boundaries.

Patch followed the pair of them out and while she was debating how to tell him she didn't want to date him, Joe said, "I'm worried about Grandma and Grandpa. How do you think they're doing?"

"Oh." As she scrambled to get her mind off how to turn him down for a date and onto Velma and Ernest, she patted Patch, who was butting her leg with his head, asking for affection. It bought her a moment to think about the question in a serious way. "Obviously, they're not getting younger, but they manage well. If you're asking about the health of the herd, it's excellent. But Ernest works as hard as a man half his age, and getting good farm help around here isn't easy." She thought about the young guys she knew who'd left Hidden Falls. "There are better paying jobs to be had in bigger cities. And Ernest has high standards. He won't put up with laziness or shoddy work."

Joe made a face. "Don't I know it. Does he still think he can treat his hands the way he was treated sixty years ago?"

Well, he'd brought it up. "Pretty much. They don't stay long."

He nodded and she imagined he'd hoped she had better news. She tried to focus on the positive. "But they've got lots of friends here. We all look out for each other."

"I know." He hesitated. "If it gets bad, will you let me know? Call me or email me? I want to help as much as I can."

So she ended up doing the very thing she'd promised herself she wouldn't do. She gave Joe her phone number and email address.

"$\mathcal{A}$nd now he has my phone number," she complained to Iris as they munched Velma's apple cake later that day.

Iris was irresistibly lured by a chance to sample Velma's apple cake, as Lauren had known she would be. They were sitting in the kitchen of her little rental house in town, only a couple of blocks from Iris and Geoff's place. It was a little more run down, but the price was reasonable, and the owner didn't mind her having pets. This was important as there was always an animal or three in residence. Most were temporary. She was fostering a couple of tortoiseshell kittens until homes could be found for them, and she was also housing a rabbit with a broken leg. At the moment, one kitten was curled up asleep in her lap. Its sister was similarly occupied on Iris's lap.

"You're like a rich man always worrying that women are only after him for his money. Maybe you need to give some of these guys more credit. There's more to you than a gorgeous face and killer body, you know." Then Iris sighed and forked up more cake. "I don't know why I don't hate you."

"So not helping."

Iris closed her eyes and chewed slowly, an expression of

intense concentration on her face. "The ginger and cinnamon are coming out as clear as anything, but there's a quiet note being played that I can't pick up. Do you think it's cardamom?"

"I just eat the cake, I don't deconstruct it."

"I miss those days," Iris sighed. "When cake was just cake. Muffins were a breakfast food, not a profit center. But those days are gone. I guess it's like you and animals. They used to be pets —now they're paying your rent. Anyway, back to you. Last time I saw Joe Benbow, he'd turned out droolworthy."

Lauren forked up more cake. "I guess. That's not the point. I'm not interested."

"If only you were gay. I have lots of nice gay female friends."

She rolled her eyes. "Even if I were, I'd still chill the matchmaking." She was terrified she'd never find anyone who saw her for who she was and not how she looked.

The kitten on Iris's lap made a *brrp* noise and tucked itself into a tighter ball. Iris looked down. "So much cuteness in one tiny package. How do you not keep them all? All these animals that you find and foster and heal?"

Lauren ran her index finger slowly over the purring bundle warming her thighs. "I suppose it's because I know there's a perfect home for every animal. Sort of like people. When it's the right match, you know instinctively. For instance, the way that kitten went straight for you."

Iris looked slightly alarmed. "I've already got crawling twins in my house. I can't handle anything more."

Lauren smiled, feeling she'd made her point. "Then it's not right, or it's the right animal but not the right time."

"Why do I have this feeling of doom—that as soon as my kids are under control, I'll have a homeless animal foisted on me?"

"Not foisted. You'll choose each other. Trust me. When it's right, you'll know."

"That's kind of how love works. With Geoff, my heart knew right away, I think, but we both let outside factors affect our behavior. Though, in fairness, with him not divorced yet and me choosing my sperm donor, we were pretty far apart."

"But true love prevailed," she said.

"I wish it would with you."

Lauren put up her hands so fast she almost forked herself in the eye. "With both Rose and Marguerite getting married this year, there's enough love in the air, thank you very much."

"So, Holly and Scott are in town this weekend. Holly's planning Marguerite's wedding and we're all meeting at Sunflower on Saturday morning for a meeting. It's at eleven a.m."

"And you're telling me this, why?"

"Because Mom's making me go along as I'll end up getting involved, and I want you there for moral support."

"And another body for Mom to assign chores to?"

"You may not be my smartest sister—that would be Paisley —but you're right up there."

THE SUNFLOWER COFFEE and Tea Company served the best coffee, muffins, and cakes in all of Hidden Falls and for miles around. The sandwiches were scrumptious and, since Kimberly Grant had begun working for Iris and had added specialty cakes, there was always someone picking up a birthday, anniversary, or congratulatory cake. But these weren't the only things that made Sunflower so special. It was the atmosphere Iris had created. The tables weren't too close together, the coffee shop was well lit, and always warm and dry no matter the weather. Sunflower was, quite simply, the meeting place of Hidden Falls.

If you wanted to find out what was going on? Head to Sunflower. Looking for a kid to mow the lawn? A local used car?

A babysitter? The latest charity or community event? Check out the community board.

The café was busy that Saturday as she walked in. Her mom had insisted she spend part of her precious day off helping plan her sister's wedding. She lived within walking distance of Sunflower and she'd worn hiking boots and brought her backpack along so that on her way home she could make a house call to a Jack Russell terrier recovering from surgery.

The smells of fresh baking and coffee lifted her mood as she entered. Her mom was already there, perusing the ads and notices, so Lauren joined her as they waited for Marguerite and Holly.

A new yoga class was starting at someone's house in a couple of weeks. She put a hand to her belly. Yoga would be good for her core, but she knew she wouldn't go. Jefferson High's drama club was selling spring baskets to raise money for their end-of-year show. That notice got a prominent place on the bulletin board, she noted, probably because Iris's husband, Geoff, was a teacher at the school and helped out with the drama club.

The local writing group also met here. Though Lauren wondered why Iris bothered having a special meeting time, since every writer in town seemed to hang out in Sunflower, nursing a single coffee and tapping away at novels, screenplays, poetry, or whatever it was they did, while making use of Iris's free Wi-Fi. She didn't seem to mind, and had been known to stop what she was doing to help brainstorm a plot point in between barista, baking, and baby-making.

Her oldest sister was a remarkable woman.

Lauren could just about manage to keep track of a couple of the stray cats and hurt rabbit she was fostering. She added her name to the spring basket order form. Iris would only force her to buy one if she didn't volunteer. Besides, the flowers would dress up the front of her small house.

Someone set the sunflower chimes to jangling and when she glanced up she saw Marguerite. The bride-to-be brought in a spatter of rain with her, some of it clinging to her curly brown hair. She shook out her umbrella and set it in the big pottery stand painted with sunflowers that their mother Daphne had made in her pottery studio. It listed slightly to one side—the leaning tower of umbrella stands—but so far it held half a dozen wet umbrellas and didn't seem in danger of falling over.

When she saw Lauren and Daphne, her face lit up. "I'm sorry I'm late. I thought the meeting was at your house, and then when Dad caught sight of me he needed me to hold the ladder for him." A hint of despair hid behind her usual sunny manner.

Lauren got a sick feeling in her stomach, as she did whenever the words *Dad* and *ladder* were used in the same sentence. Now she understood why they were meeting at Iris's café instead of at the Chance family home. "Oh, no, Mom. What's Dad building this time? Please let it not involve anything electrical or plumbing related." Jack Chance was a home handyman who had much more enthusiasm than skill.

"Don't worry. It's just a sagging gutter that needed fixing."

She relaxed slightly. The trouble with Dad was that one project invariably led to another, usually a more complicated one. He could easily decide, while fixing the gutter, that they needed a new roof. Unfortunately, his favorite tool was the sledgehammer. He liked to tear things down and then figure out how to fix them. She could imagine the home where she grew up roofless in the rain while he tried to figure out how to build a roof.

They settled at a table and Lauren said, "You sit. I'll get coffees. What do you want?"

"I'll just have a green tea," Marguerite said.

"Make it two," their mother agreed.

She made her way up to the front, where Kimberly, her

brother James's girlfriend, was manning the front counter. "Hi Lauren, what can I get you?"

"Green tea for Mom and Marguerite, and I'll have a chai latte." Holly came in and joined the other two.

As Kimberly started on the drinks, Iris came out of the kitchen with a fresh tray of tarts that looked and smelled wickedly good. She greeted Lauren and said, "You have to try these. One of Kimberly's Canadian recipes. Butter tarts." She didn't wait for a reply, but put four of the tarts on a plate and handed them over to Lauren.

"Any idea what Holly drinks?"

"Americano," her sister said, without even pausing to think. So she added that to her order.

Kimberly, meanwhile, was looking behind Lauren with a slightly puzzled expression. As she passed over the tray of drinks she asked, "Does that guy know you? He hasn't taken his eyes off you since you came over here."

Lauren didn't turn around, but felt her shoulders tighten. Iris glanced back and shook her head. "Guy's a stranger in town. You'll get used to it. There's just something about Lauren. It happens all the time. Next thing you know, he'll be singing us the love song he composed in her honor. Or going out to buy her flowers, which he'll present on bended knee." She nudged her shoulder against Kim's. "Once your vanity gets used to the blow, it's pretty funny."

Not to me.

"Wow. It's because you're so pretty, I guess," Kim said, looking impressed.

As she carried the tray of drinks and tarts back to the table, she made sure not to look in the direction Kimberly had indicated.

She greeted both her sister and Holly with a hug, and they

all sat, crowding around a table. "Another one of Kim's additions to the menu," she said as she picked up a butter tart.

Her mom picked up another. "That girl arriving in Hidden Falls is not helping my waistline," Daphne complained as she bit into the tart. Then she moaned, sounding like a woman in a porn movie. "Oh, oh, that is so good."

Lauren bit into her own tart and understood the impulse. The tart was still warm and gooey, with butter and brown sugar and raisins and who knew what else inside perfect flaky pastry.

Iris came over with her apron off and a coffee in her hand. She took a detour on the way, and Lauren could see out of the corner of her eye that she'd paused behind the young man whose eyes had been boring into Lauren since she'd arrived.

"Oh, it's good to get off my feet," she said, pulling up a chair to join them.

"Was he writing a poem?" Daphne asked, obviously as aware as the other two of the young stranger's interest.

"A pencil drawing of our beautiful sister," Iris answered. "Pretty good, too. I always feel like the ugly stepsister around you."

She shook her head. "Trust me, it's a curse. Not a blessing."

Lauren barely noticed the welcome chimes. So many customers were coming and going with a flutter of raindrops and opening and closing of umbrellas, the putting on and taking off of rain jackets. But when her mother half rose from her chair with a smile of welcome, she turned to look. Even as she recognized the bundled figure coming in through the door, raindrops clinging to his tousled hair, her mother was saying, "Why, that's Joe Benbow," and then louder, so he could hear her, "Joe! I heard you were back in town. Come give me a hug."

With a nod that took in the five women, Joe obliged. Even as she said, "Come join us, and tell us what you've been up to," he was saying, "Can't stop, I need to put up a notice."

Lauren could see that something was wrong. His eyes looked grave and his smile strained. She asked, "Is everything all right with Ernest and Velma?"

He nodded, but the worry didn't fade. "Two of the calves are missing."

"What?" She'd seen those sweet babies only yesterday. "What happened? And how long have they been gone?" They'd be so hungry, and lost, and scared.

Joe said, "Grandma and Grandpa trailered them over to their neighbors down the road who raise some of the calves." He glanced at Lauren. "The Emersons. About five miles away."

She nodded. She'd visited their small farm a few times.

"I don't know what happened. Grandpa thinks the back gate wasn't attached properly, but somewhere between their place and the Emersons', two of the calves either jumped or fell out. We've been hollering and calling and walking back and forth up the road around where Grandpa thinks they went missing, but nobody's seen them."

She was already on her feet. "But surely somebody's heard them? They'll be hungry, and bawling."

He shook his head, looking helpless. It happened on a lonely stretch of road, with lots of paths leading down to the river. "I thought I'd put a notice here, in case anyone sees them. But I have to get back, got to keep looking."

She said to the table of women, "Sorry to go so soon, but I'm going to help them look."

"Of course you are," said her mom. "I'll run home and grab Jack and anybody else I can find, and we'll head out to join you."

"I can't ask you to do that—" Joe began.

"Honey, you've been away from Hidden Falls too long. This is what we do. We help each other."

Iris said, "When I get off work, if they're still missing, Geoff or I will look after the twins, and the other one will come and join the search party." She reached out her hand. "Give me that notice. I'll make sure it gets the best spot on the bulletin board."

He nodded, and from beneath his jacket produced a hand-lettered sign.

"Good luck," she said, and walked toward the coffee bar, the sign fluttering in her hand. No doubt she was going for a thumbtack.

Daphne said, "You go with Joe, Lauren. It will save time. I'll go and pick up your father. And Cooper was planning to drop by. We'll bring him along, too."

Marguerite and Holly began packing up. Marguerite said, "Between all of us, we'll find your babies. I'll drop Holly back at home. Alex is working today, but I'll join the search."

"So will I," Holly said. Lauren would have preferred not to ride with Joe, but she could hardly argue with her mother, not with Joe standing right there. Besides, her mom was right. The day was cold and wet, and the calves were in danger from predators, accidents, and starvation. They might weigh seventy pounds each, but they were only babies.

Swiftly, she tucked herself back into her own rain jacket. Her Blundstone boots would be up for the job, though her jeans would soon be soaked.

He was about to open the door when Iris said, "Wait." She held a Thermos and a stack of takeout cups. "Hot coffee," she said. "You'll need it."

Lauren took the Thermos and cups and Joe opened the door for her. They headed back out into the rain. She pulled the hood of her rain jacket over her hair and the pair of them jogged, splashing through puddles, to his SUV.

They nearly collided on the way to the passenger door, until she realized he planned to open it for her. She held back and let him complete his chivalrous gesture, even though they'd have saved a minute or so if he'd left her to open her own door. By the time she had her seatbelt on, he had jogged around the vehicle and was climbing in the driver's side.

As he backed out, he said, "I can't tell you how much my grandparents will appreciate your help. They're beside themselves with worry, and of course, blaming themselves."

She knew only too well how much Velma and Ernest cared about their animals. And, while Ernest had little tolerance for mistakes made by people working for him, he had zero for himself.

She didn't want to sit in silence all the way to the Benbow farm, but she couldn't think of anything to talk about. If he lived here, they could chat endlessly about local politics, the current debate raging on whether the high school football team's need for new uniforms was more important than the drama department's wish for a larger costume budget. Her dad's suggestion that the school put on a musical about football so the uniforms could serve both purposes hadn't been well received. But Joe didn't live here, so he probably wouldn't care about those things. If she brought them up, he might conclude they were a bunch of hicks, which he probably thought anyway now that he lived in San Diego.

As the silence stretched, making the rain pounding the roof sound louder, she fell back on, "How long are you here for?" She'd only asked the question for something to say, but the way he turned to glance at her made her wonder if she'd accidentally raised a sore subject.

The expression in his eyes was troubled. "Honestly, I don't know. I brought my dad's ashes home to scatter them, and I was going to leave in a couple of days, but now that I'm here, especially today, I want to stay longer and help."

She nodded. Then, since he'd brought up the subject, she said, "I was sorry to hear about your dad."

In the pause before he answered, the rain grew heavier. He

had the windshield wipers on full speed, but it was like peering underwater through a rushing stream. "Thanks. I had him cremated overseas, but I thought he'd have wanted to end up here, with family." He blew out a breath. "I don't even know if that's what he wanted. Maybe I should have scattered his ashes on the island where he lived, but it didn't seem like he had much of a life there, and I thought Grandma and Grandpa would want him laid to rest back here."

She felt the urge to comfort, wanted to lay her hand over his where it gripped the steering wheel too hard. Velma and Ernest had lost a son, but Joe had lost a father. A father he'd barely known. "I'm sure they're happy to have him home," she said softly.

"Well, thing is, they assumed I'd already done something with him and I could tell they were relieved. I don't have the heart to tell them he's here."

"Here?"

He jutted his chin behind him. "In the back."

She turned to look and there was a cardboard box in the back of the SUV. She wondered what it felt like, driving around with your father's mortal remains, and hoped she'd never have to find out. "I'm so sorry," she said again. "It must be hard for you." Not only figuring out what to do with the ashes, but coming to terms with his loss.

"Hard for all of us. They always hoped my dad would take over the farm." He gave a low, bitter laugh. "That didn't happen. Then they pinned their hopes on me." He swerved to miss a deep pothole in the road, now a huge mud puddle. "But I have another life."

She had a sudden memory of him as a teenager, shirt off, working in the yard alongside his grandfather, his skin golden from the sun, his jeans low on his hips. She blinked the vision away. "You always seemed happy here."

"I was, but I had itchy feet, too, wanted to get out of this small town and see things."

"And have you?"

He glanced sideways at her as though he thought she was teasing. Then saw her question was serious. He seemed to ponder. "Sure. I guess I always wanted more excitement. Raising a herd of dairy cows wasn't a path I would've chosen for myself. I wasn't born to it—not like Ernest—so I struck out on my own. I've been a full-time firefighter now for seven years and, truth is, a fire station is its own family, its own small town. Ernest and Velma did a helluva lot more than my parents did to raise me, teach me some kind of values, give me a place that always felt like home. I owe them everything."

She could hear the guilt in his tone. Knowing Ernest and Velma would never want him to feel that way, she said, "They are so proud of you. You know they would never, ever want to hold you back from your dreams."

"But how long can they manage the farm? How long can they keep going without decent help?"

She wasn't going to lie to him. He was right. "Honestly, I don't know." They were turning in to the Benbow farm now.

Joe said, "I'll let them know we're back, and that more help is on its way. Maybe they've even found the calves by now."

He pulled into the gravel parking area near the house and they both got out. "Grandma?" Joe yelled as he entered the house, Lauren right behind him. They stayed in the mudroom so as not to have to take off their boots and Velma came out from the kitchen, Patch trailing her and then rushing up to Joe to greet him. Joe gave him an absent pat on the head and the dog headed to Lauren, who dropped to her knees to give him a proper greeting.

"I'm more worried about Ernest than those calves," Velma said. "He got so worked up. He blames himself. You know how hard he is on everyone else, but he's even harder on himself. I told him he's no good to anybody if he gets sick out there in the rain and cold, but you know that man, he never listens. He'll be eighty next year and he still thinks he's twenty-five."

Joe nodded. "First thing we're going to do is find Grandpa and send him home. Lauren's here, half her family seems to be on their way, and I put up a notice at Sunflower. Don't you worry, Grandma, we'll find those calves. But we'll find Grandpa first, and if I have to throw him over my shoulder and bring him home in a firefighter carry, I will."

Lauren hid her smile in Patch's fur. She wondered if Joe had any idea how much like his grandfather he was turning out to be.

"Bless you, both of you," Velma said. "Lauren, I know you're going to find them, or at least do your best. It was such a silly thing. I don't know how we came to not latch the back of the trailer properly."

Joe said, "Hey, it happens to all of us. I'll check that latch myself, and make sure it's working properly." She liked the way he cast doubt on the trailer's locking mechanism. "You call my cell phone if you hear anything."

"I will, but the reception's terrible out here."

"Don't worry, Grandma. We've got this."

She liked the way he included her as part of his team.

CHAPTER 4

a s they plunged back into the rain and jogged to the SUV, Lauren let Joe open her door for her. He'd never learned those manners from his dad. That old-fashioned chivalry came from his grandfather. She wondered if he even knew how much like Ernest he was. She'd seen the determination and the command and she knew beyond a doubt that if he had to stay up all night searching, calling until he was hoarse, he wouldn't stop until the calves were found.

They headed down the road a few miles until they spotted Ernest's gray pickup and trailer parked at the side of the road. They pulled in behind him and both climbed out. There was no sign of Ernest in the truck. She stopped and listened, but couldn't hear the older man's voice. But then, it was hard to hear anything over the pounding of the rain. Velma was right to be worried about her husband; he shouldn't be out for long in this weather.

There was a track leading away from the road but Ernest might just as easily have gone walking on ahead. She said, "Why don't I explore down this track while you drive ahead a little bit and look for Ernest?" At this point, they were both more worried about Joe's grandfather than about the young calves.

"You sure? Maybe you should take the SUV while I head off down the track."

He was being chivalrous again, making sure she stayed dry. She shook her head at him. "Do you really think your grandfather is going to listen to me? If I find him, I'll message you, but if you find him, you can get him into your vehicle and then come back and get me."

He seemed to see the sense in her plan and nodded. "At least take the hot coffee with you."

"I haven't got cold yet. I'm barely even wet. Being a vet, especially a country vet, may not be as dangerous as being a firefighter, but believe me, I'm used to roughing it. If anyone needs hot coffee, it's going to be Ernest." And before he could say another word, she headed down the track.

She didn't hear the SUV drive away, but then, with the sound of raindrops splashing against already wet leaves and bouncing off the hood of her rain jacket, she couldn't hear much of anything. Unfortunately, she wouldn't hear Ernest or even a crying calf until she was close up. She glanced up at the sky, but it was heavy and gray with rain clouds that showed no sign of moving away.

A raindrop hit her in the eye.

She resisted the urge to shout for Ernest, knowing her voice wouldn't carry far and she'd wear it out quickly. She decided to use her eyes and her ears before yelling herself hoarse. Cell phone service was patchy at best in this part of Hidden Falls, so she had no way of getting hold of Ernest other than to find him.

She headed down along the track until it hit the edge of the river. There was no sign of man or cow.

She squinted against the wet and peered left and right. She spent a few fruitless minutes more, as though the three of them might wander into view, but the only wildlife she saw was a pair of ducks paddling in a quiet eddy at the river's edge.

She pictured all the little tracks and lanes that led off this stretch of highway. It was going to be a long day.

And it was. By late afternoon, a dozen people had joined in the search, half of them part of her family, as well as Benbow friends and neighbors. When Joe found him, Ernest had refused to go home, even after Joe yelled at him not to be a fool. He'd yelled right back and after they both bellowed at each other, they stomped away in opposite directions, their postures straight and stiff, both equally red in the face.

Lauren might have laughed at how very much alike they were if she hadn't been so worried that Ernest was pushing himself too hard. At least he accepted a cup of coffee, even if he did curse himself for an old fool while he drank it.

She was now riding with Marguerite in her sister's old red truck. The search party had been back and forth between the Benbow farm and the Emersons'. Now they were expanding the search another mile up the road. Joe had taken charge of the search party and it was clear he was used to command. Did his fire station also do search and rescue? She suspected, from the way he gave orders so confidently, that it did.

"If only it would stop raining," she said, beginning to despair.

"We're going to find them," Marguerite said. "I feel it."

Lauren only hoped they would find the calves in time. They'd set up a command center at the kitchen table of the Benbow kitchen and Joe put the volunteers into parties of two and assigned them an area. The idea was that if two people found a calf, or both calves, the second person could run back to the road and alert the rest of the team.

As they headed down yet another trail that led off the road

and down toward the river, she said, "Sorry our wedding planning meeting got interrupted."

"Doesn't matter. There's lots of time." Marguerite had to be the calmest engaged woman she'd ever seen. She was so relaxed she made Lauren want to take up yoga and organic gardening. She only wished their sister Rose were half as relaxed.

"I wasn't sure you'd be the marrying kind."

Marguerite seemed to ponder the remark while peering through the bushes along her side of the trail. "I didn't think I was the marrying kind, either, but Alexei is much more traditional and it means a lot to him and his family."

"Are you really going to do the *My Big Fat Greek Wedding* thing?" She'd never met Alexei's family, but the stories that Rose and Marguerite told made her think they were in for an interesting experience.

Marguerite turned to her. "You have no idea. I would have thought that with two of her sons getting married, Alexei's mom would only be half as involved in each wedding. It makes sense, right?"

"Make sense to me. Divide and conquer and all that." She caught a flash of movement on her side of the trail, but it was only a grouse huddling in a tree for shelter. "I'm guessing you're not dividing or conquering."

"That woman has so much energy she makes our mom look like a slacker. Rose is both harder to get hold of and tougher to deal with, so I'm getting the brunt of the help. And when she gets going, she forgets to speak in English so I'm not even sure what I've agreed to." She paused and put a hand on Lauren's arm, stopping her on the trail.

Lauren turned to her in surprise.

Marguerite said, "Maybe this isn't the best moment to ask you this, but at least we're alone. I wanted to ask if you would be my maid of honor."

She felt a flutter of happiness in her chest, swiftly followed by mild panic. "Wow. I'm flattered. But aren't you closer to—"

"No," Marguerite said quite firmly. "If you don't want to do it, you just have to say no, but please don't try and make an excuse as to why someone else would be better suited. You are the one I want. Maybe you don't want to be the center of attention, and I understand that, but it's important to me and I wanted to ask you first." Wet black curls made question marks against her forehead and cheeks.

Lauren knew how foolish she would sound, telling a bride that she didn't want to be her maid of honor because she didn't want to put on a pretty dress and have her hair done and wear makeup. How could she explain that she didn't want to be put on display and not come across as incredibly vain? It was Marguerite's day. Of course she, the bride, would be the center of attention.

And yet, she imagined all those eyes on her and it was only because she loved her sister so much that she said, "Of course I want to be your maid of honor. I'm so happy you asked me."

They hugged awkwardly in the middle of the trail, torn between laughter and tears. Marguerite said, "I'm not going to be one of those monster brides who makes you wear some godawful dress. You can choose whatever you want."

"I haven't been shopping in so long. Maybe we could go together?"

"I'd love that. We'll make a day of it—go to Portland or Seattle and hopefully find dresses for both of us."

"Just the two of us? Don't you want the rest of the sisters to be bridesmaids, too?"

"Honestly, I'm trying to keep this wedding small."

Lauren chuckled. "When you're one of eleven kids, and you include husbands and wives, boyfriends and girlfriends, there is no such thing as small. Plus, I'm guessing the Greeks don't really go in for small weddings."

Marguerite shuddered. "Originally, his parents wanted us to have the wedding in Greece, so all the Vasilopolous uncles and aunts and cousins could help celebrate. Luckily Alex talked them out of it. I think a some relatives might be coming from Greece, but he doesn't have a huge family here. Friends, though." Marguerite sounded a little overwhelmed.

"Did you think about eloping?"

"Only about a hundred times. And that was during the weekend we spent at his parents' house."

"Well, as your maid of honor, I will do my best to help this thing run smoothly. But, of course, you're in good hands with Holly."

"I know. She's the best. She told me I could give Alexei's mother her phone number, but I like her too much to do that. Besides, she might refuse to plan the wedding after a conversation with my future mother-in-law. And then where would I be?"

"You'll be fine. I'm sure Holly's dealt with tougher customers than you could ever be."

"I wonder when she's getting married. That house she and Prescott are building in The Mission must be nearly finished, even by Scott's exacting standards."

"I bet they're waiting so they can have the wedding there."

Marguerite shook her head. "I picture Prescott booking somewhere very far away from where he lives or works, so he won't be disrupted by noise or commotion."

"That poor guy. It must've been so hard for him growing up in our crazy family, the way he craves order and quiet."

"No harder than it was for any of us. The boys tease you endlessly about being so pretty and the way every guy in town wrote poems or painted pictures or composed songs in your honor, sometimes all three at once, and that couldn't have been easy." She stopped to disentangle a blackberry thorn from her jeans. "I think my favorite was the sky-writing guy. It's not every day you look up and see *I love you, Lauren* floating above your home like a message from God."

Lauren groaned. "Don't you start. You're as bad as the boys."

"And poor Paisley, being the brainiac of the family. I wish we hadn't teased her so much, or made her help us with our homework when she was years younger than we were."

"I know. I was so proud of myself when I taught her to read. She was only three years old and she read all my Harry Potter's, my whole Series of Unfortunate Events, and those animal books I loved. In fact, by the time she was six, I think she'd read every book in our house."

Marguerite stiffened and raised her head. "Hey. Was that an animal cry?"

They exchanged a glance, and both began to run. "Cows? Baby cows?" Marguerite yelled as they pounded down the trail.

Now Lauren could hear it, too, and it definitely sounded like an animal in distress. Of course it could be a deer, or a sheep separated from its flock, but to her ear, the cry sounded bovine.

They followed the sounds and discovered both of the calves.

One had somehow caught itself in a blackberry thicket and the thick, green, thorny vines had acted like barbed wire. The more the calf had panicked and tried to escape, the tighter it got stuck. It had also sustained an injury to its head and a flap of hide was loose. That would need to be stitched. The second calf stood by, looking wet and forlorn but unharmed.

They both cried louder when they saw Lauren and Marguerite and she could've sworn that if they'd been people, they would've been saying, "Thank God you're here. What took you so long?"

She went forward, her eye already running over the trapped calf, which looked at her with its big, liquid brown eyes and cried again piteously. She said to Marguerite, "You go back, and as soon as you get a cell signal, call Joe. You can tell him that both animals are alive and basically healthy as far as I can tell. Whoever comes should bring gardening shears or wire cutters, something to help free the calf." She was already taking off her backpack and unzipping it to retrieve her first-aid kit as Marguerite went running back up the path.

She did her best to soothe the animals, talking to them and stroking them. At her calming tone, she was able to get the trapped calf to stop struggling at least. In less than half an hour she heard the sounds she'd been waiting for.

"Over here!"

Joe's voice rang out. "Lauren! Thank God. How are they?"

"I think they're going to be fine."

At the sight of Joe and Ernest, who arrived just behind his grandson, panting heavily from the run, the cows cried even more piteously. The older man glanced at Lauren with a question in his eyes. "They'll be fine, as soon as we get them back home and fed. The stuck one's going to need some stitches, but they're more hungry and scared than hurt."

He simply nodded, but she could see how relieved he was. While she did her best to soothe the animal and Ernest talked to it in his gruff way, Joe wielded a hefty pair of shears. Some of the brambles were so thick she could see his biceps bulge under his jacket. When the calf was freed, Joe picked it up and carried it, even though it must have weighed seventy or eighty pounds. She and Ernest led the second one up the path with the rope he'd brought.

She tried not to melt as she watched Joe carry the injured calf up the path with all the care he would show to a child he'd rescued from a burning building.

When they got back to the farm, Joe insisted on sending Ernest into the house where it was warm, while he assisted her in spite of her arguments that she could manage alone. In fact, it was nice to have his help, as he was able to hold the injured calf still as she cleaned and stitched up its wound. "It's a clean cut," she said as she worked. "Should heal just fine."

He had nice hands, she thought idly. Capable, with strong, square-tipped fingers. He didn't fuss or fidget, or chatter away, but simply held the calf and made her job easier. She forgot to be nervous around him as she, like the calf, began to trust that she was in safe hands.

CHAPTER 5

*J*oe made absolutely certain to keep his distance. Which wasn't easy, given that he was holding a struggling calf while she treated its injuries.

He didn't let their hands accidentally touch and did his best to stay out of her personal space. He wished he could apologize for his teenaged behavior, but that would probably only make her uncomfortable. If he saw a young recruit at the fire station acting the way he had, he'd haul the kid aside and lecture him about stalking and inappropriate behavior. He didn't think his own behavior had reached the level of stalking, but he'd made a nice young girl feel uncomfortable and in his own books that was still a crime.

His best bet was to make his current behavior an apology for his past. He'd make sure to keep his distance from her, never make personal comments or attempt to be alone with her. He was going to treat Lauren like any other girl he'd met when he came to stay with his grandparents in the summers—like any of the other Chance girls, a family acquaintance, no more.

And if he still thought she was the most beautiful woman he'd ever seen, and if his awkward adolescent crush hadn't completely gone away, he would keep that information firmly to himself.

His plan began to work almost immediately. Lauren started out a little uncomfortable and seemed nervous with only the two of them and the calf in the barn, alone but for the other animals. But she soon grew so engrossed in what she was doing, talking softly to her patient, which had the usual effect of calming the poor thing, and he was so respectful about keeping his distance, that he could sense her beginning to relax.

When she was done, he said, "I'll take her back and feed and settle her. See you back at the house."

She was packing her things away and glanced up as he hefted the calf into his arms once more. "I'll come with you. I want to make sure she eats okay before I sign off on my patient."

He merely nodded and kept walking. She caught up to him and was able to witness the reunion as all the young calves called out a greeting as the stray was returned. The little gal took her food without any problems and with a final nod, Lauren said she was satisfied.

They headed up to the house together.

The rain had finally stopped, but the gravel path was more puddle than gravel. For something to say, he said, "I'll have to fill these holes while I'm here."

"You have a lot to do in a short time."

"Yeah." He felt guilty at only being able to stay for a few weeks, when he could see how much there was to do on the farm and how much his grandparents could use his help. Plus, when he'd lost his father, they'd lost their only son. His dad wasn't much of a dad or a son, but while Frank Benbow had been alive, there'd always been that hope that he might change. Figure out what he was missing and come home. Now it was too late.

"I don't know what to do with him," he said, surprised that

he'd said the words aloud, and to Lauren of all people. "My dad, I mean."

He heard a scatter of gravel, as though her step had halted and then started up again. "You probably don't want to leave him in the back of the SUV."

He tilted up his head to look at where the stars would be if this were a clear night. "Maybe I wasn't thinking clearly, I don't know. I thought he'd want to be scattered here, in Hidden Falls, where he grew up. I thought Grandma and Grandpa might want some kind of a memorial or something."

"And they don't?"

He shook his head. "You know what Grandma said to me? She said she was glad they weren't burying him on the farm, because then they'd never be able to sell it." He sighed, feeling the weight of disappointed expectations press down on his shoulders. "I wish they didn't have to sell. They love this place. But with no one to take over and run it, how long can they keep it going?"

They stayed silent for a moment or two. Water splashed over the top of his boot as he trod through a puddle. After a moment, she said, "It's not your fault that your father never wanted to be a farmer, and it's not your fault that you've moved away and become a firefighter. Your grandparents are so proud of you. You shouldn't feel guilty."

"But I do." He felt guilty every time he came here and saw them getting a little bit older, a little bit slower, finding the work a little bit harder. He felt guilty because he loved them and wanted them to be able to keep the farm. He felt guilty because maybe, when he had been younger, he'd believed that one day he'd take over and become a dairy farmer. He cringed inside as he recalled, in the worst days of his infatuation, his fantasy of himself and Lauren running this place.

After he left Hidden Falls, he'd imagined Lauren Chance being spotted by some lucky talent scout and ending up at a top modeling agency, living in Paris or London or New York. He'd mentally braced himself for the day he'd see her photograph on the cover of a magazine. Or maybe she'd become an actress and he'd see her on the big screen. But, it wasn't she who had left town and never come back; it was Joe. She was here, helping farmers like his grandparents, settled and presumably happy in Hidden Falls.

"Please don't tell my grandparents. I'll figure out something to do with his ashes."

They carried on a few more steps in silence and then she said, softly, "I'm not sure it's your grandparents who need a memorial service, or some kind of closure. I think it's you."

That stopped him in his tracks. He actually stopped walking as the truth of her words sank deep. She was right. He hadn't been able to toss his father's remains in the ocean half a world away where no one would care about him or remember him. He wanted to feel that his mortal remains would end up as part of the place where he'd grown up.

Home.

Joe's home.

It hadn't meant much to his dad for a lot of his life, but he had a feeling that Frank, like him, had always believed that one day he'd end up back here. "When my ship comes in," he used to say. Well, his ship never had come in, but at least he was home.

"I didn't know your dad very well—hardly at all—but he must've had a special place here, someplace that meant something to him? Maybe there was a place you both cared about?"

"Yeah," Joe said. "We did have a special place. He took me up the trail to the falls a few times. They were some of the best we ever had."

And he knew in that moment how he was going to say good-bye.

~

THE DOOR OPENED and light spilled out, and his grandmother, who'd obviously been watching for them, called out, "Come on in, you two. I've got fresh coffee on and a pot of stew. Let's get you dried off and warmed up." He stood back to let Lauren go ahead of him and when she stepped into the mudroom, Velma threw her arms around her, wet raincoat and all. "Thank you for finding those calves and bringing them back."

Lauren hugged his grandma, then pulled away gently. She peeled off her wet coat and hung it on one of the hooks, along with a number of other dripping coats.

"They're both absolutely fine." Then she sniffed the air. "Oh, my, that stew smells good. I didn't realize how hungry I was." Her hair was damp, her cheeks reddened from the cold, wet rain, but her eyes glowed. His probably did, too. They'd found the calves and got them home safely. It felt good.

He hung up his own rain jacket, making sure to put it on the other side of the room so she wouldn't think his jacket was trying to make time with hers. He changed into dry shoes while his grandmother gave Lauren a pair of clean sweat pants and some hand-knit slippers to wear in the house.

He washed up while Lauren was led off by Grandma to change. They all met up in the kitchen, where it sounded like an impromptu party was going on. Grandma, like a true farm wife, could feed the multitudes practically at a moment's notice. Her stew bubbled on the stove, and she'd taken a couple of fruit pies out of the freezer that were waiting to go into the oven. Half a dozen loaves of French bread sat on the counter, the only food that came from the grocery store.

His grandmother fussed over both of them, insisting on pouring the coffee herself.

When he walked into the big living room, his fingers gripped the handle of the coffee mug hard. James and Joshua, the Chance twins, were both there, along with their younger brother, Cooper. Of all the people he'd like to avoid in this town, next to Lauren, these three topped his list. On that never-to-be-forgotten night when his hormones had overcome his common sense, these three had mocked him unmercifully. Ben and Evan and Prescott had joined in, but it was the three younger boys who'd been the worst and, he was sure, were the ones who'd shared the story around town.

Well, he reminded himself, he was grown up now, a professional firefighter, and he lived a long way from these clowns. Plus, this was his grandparents' house. He wasn't a skinny, oversensitive boy any longer. He could kick them out if he needed to.

He liked that mental image a lot.

After that short inner pep talk, he realized that James was walking with the aid of a cane and that Cooper, who still appeared to have the mental age of about thirteen, was teasing him about something. As though feeling his gaze on them, Cooper glanced over his way and beckoned.

"Hey, Joe, did you hear about how my brother here got wounded in the line of duty?" His eyes were dancing with mischief and he wore a crooked grin the chicks probably dug and which made Joe want to punch him in the mouth.

There was nothing funny about being wounded while doing your civic duty, and no one knew that better than a firefighter. Feeling a sudden and unexpected kinship with James Chance, he walked over to the group of three.

"Hey man, I'm sorry to hear that." He wouldn't ask what happened because, in his experience, sometimes the trauma of a recollected gun battle, a fire, a drug bust gone wrong, was the last thing the officers involved ever wanted to talk about. Instead, he said, "I hope you heal soon."

"Thanks," James said shortly. Joe could see his instinct had been right and James didn't want to talk about the cause of his injury. He couldn't believe that not only Cooper, but Josh too wouldn't let it go. Didn't twins have some kind of bond where they protected each other? Josh seemed more like Cooper's twin, the way the pair of them were giggling and snorting.

James glared at them. "I apologize for my two brothers here. They were dicks when they were teenagers and they haven't grown up."

"Want me to toss them out?"

All three brothers looked at him and, if they were expecting to see the weedy sixteen-year-old who'd made a fool of himself, they were obviously reconsidering their opinions. He didn't like to boast, but he'd filled out a lot since then, and he worked out most days. Mostly so he could do his job properly, but he liked being fit and able to handle whatever a callout threw at him.

"No. But I appreciate the offer." He eyed his brothers with disfavor. "Maybe later."

It would've ended there if his grandmother hadn't come up and put her hand on James's shoulder. "James. I'm so glad you're here. I hear your wound's taking longer to heal than the doctors had hoped? Perhaps you should sit down—" Then, as though she wished she hadn't spoken those words, she said, "Oh, how foolish of me, of course you can't. I could get you a cushion."

Cooper and Josh seemed to find this exquisitely funny. "Yeah, bro, would you like a cushion for your sore tush?" Cooper asked with glee.

"Thanks, Mrs. Benbow. But I prefer to stand." Then he turned to Joe. "Since you obviously haven't heard, and my brothers aren't going to shut up about it until you do, I got shot in the butt."

"While saving a young man's life." Grandma glared at the two other Chance boys. "Which is more than either of you have ever done. You should be ashamed of yourselves, teasing your brother when he's recovering from his injuries."

She walked away then and Josh, instead of looking properly ashamed of himself, said to Joe as soon as she was out of hearing, "We've got it on film. Luckily, I have a friend at the cable TV station and for fifty bucks I got a copy of the news footage. If you want to come over sometime, I'll show it to you."

There were two things Joe couldn't believe here. First, James's own twin brother was being an insensitive asshat. Second, and even more interesting, it seemed they'd forgotten all about his foolish younger days. Or, more likely, James's recent injury had eclipsed his youthful folly.

However, there was a brotherhood among cops and firefighters and that came first. "However it happened, your brother showed a lot of bravery."

"Thanks, man," James said quietly.

With no one willing to give them the reaction they wanted, the little brothers headed off, probably looking for somebody else to mock.

James said, "So, how long are you here for?"

It was a question he was getting a lot lately. He still had no answer. He fell back on the same one he'd given Lauren. "Three more weeks. Maybe I can stretch it to four. I took compassionate leave and my vacation."

James nodded. He understood. "I was sorry to hear about your father."

"Thanks."

"Look, our volunteer fire department needs some new drills. I know it's a lot to ask when you're only here for a few weeks, but the fire department falls under my department and, frankly, they suck. Would you consider giving them an afternoon of training?"

Hidden Falls wasn't a big city and the community relied on their volunteer fire department. He knew as well as anyone that volunteers required a certain number of hours of training every year and he was professional enough to understand that if a fire broke out, they needed to be ready to go, everybody knowing what to do, and how to do it. There was no time to figure it out once the heat was literally on. He didn't really have time, not with all there was to do around the farm, but what if his grandparents had a fire? He'd want to know the volunteers were up to speed.

He nodded slowly. "Sure. I'll make some time."

James looked sincerely grateful. "That would be great."

They arranged that he'd come by the local fire station that very Saturday afternoon and give them a drill.

By the time his grandmother, ably assisted by Iris, dished up dinner, he no longer felt awkward in the presence of the Chance family. Maybe everybody had put the past behind them. Well, probably not Lauren, as she still seemed a little skittish around him, but if he kept his distance and acted cool, she might stop thinking of him as a teenager with an awful crush.

Hopefully she'd never figure out he was now a thirty-year-old man with an awful crush.

At least now he was better at hiding it, and understood better that some crushes are just plain hopeless.

CHAPTER 6

*T*he lost calves had given her a reprieve, but Lauren was still picked up by her mom the next day so she could attend the rescheduled meeting of the wedding planners. She might have refused, having lost her Saturday to the calf hunt, but now that she was Marguerite's maid of honor, she felt she should be there for her sister.

They caught up for a few minutes over coffees and then Holly unzipped her canvas backpack and removed a laptop. Her fingers flew over the keys for a moment, and then she said, "I thought we'd meet here, and just catch up. Marguerite's wedding planning is well underway and I have to tell you, it's a pleasure to work with a bride who is so easy going." Holly had first met the family when she was working for a horrible boss who wanted the famous architect Prescott Chance to design him a house. In the end, her boss hadn't ended up with a house, but Holly, to all the family's satisfaction, had ended up with Prescott.

They were the match that no one saw coming, Lauren thought, looking at the lively, animated face, the wild corkscrew curls that rain and mist had intensified. No matter how hard she tried, Holly always looked as though she had just thrown her clothes together in a hurry. Lauren suspected that most of the time she had. In comparison, Prescott was the most calm, unhurried man you could ever meet. He always looked as though he'd just stepped out of a Prada store and hadn't even sat down yet. Still, they were the perfect match for each other. It was enough to make a perennially single younger sister feel envious.

When Holly had helped plan her oldest brother, Evan, and his fiancée, Caitlyn's, wedding, she'd been so good at it that she'd decided to start her own wedding planning business. She never boasted, but Prescott boasted on her behalf— her business was growing all the time, partly because she had planned the fourth wedding of her notoriously difficult former boss, the industrialist Alastair Rupert. That assignment had been tough, and even the irrepressibly sunny Holly had nearly lost her temper dealing with the difficult and contradicting demands of Alastair Rupert and his young starlet bride.

Iris pulled up another chair and squeezed in around the table. "Have I missed anything?" She looked around the circle of faces. Holly smiled at her. "No. I was only saying what a pleasure it is planning Marguerite's wedding. A nice, simple backyard party with an easy going bride and groom."

Iris laughed. "Unlike your client, our other sister Rose?" Marguerite's wedding was set for early June, when the weather would hopefully be sunny as it was going to be held in the Chance family's back yard, catered by her fiancé's Greek food truck, and as casual and relaxed as she could make it.

Rose Chance had also hired Holly and was planning a much higher end wedding for the following spring. Holly, always diplomatic, said, "Rose is a great client too. She knows exactly what she wants.

Daphne said, "Considering you and Rose are sisters, you couldn't be more different. You both turned out like your names. Rose is like a bouquet of hothouse roses and you're like a field of daisies. Both are beautiful, but how did they come out of the same garden?"

Marguerite laughed. "I know. Rose's last vacation was at a five-star hotel and spa in Rome, while mine was a trekking expedition on the Pacific Coast Trail." She shops on Rodeo Drive and I prefer thrift stores or clothing made from sustainable natural materials from a women's co-op."

Holly said, "You might find you're more alike than you think. Both of you are trying to incorporate some Greek traditions into your ceremonies, and both of you are really into family. It's nice to see." She beamed at them all. One of Holly's nicest qualities was her genuine enthusiasm. "We're so far along with the planning, I really wanted to talk details. I know you didn't love the idea of getting married under a tent awning, but we have to be prepared in case of rain."

Marguerite didn't look as excited as Holly did, which was weird since it was her wedding. As maid of honor, Lauren was about to ask what was bothering her when Marguerite took a breath and said, "I think we need to make a couple of changes."

Holly glanced up from her notes. "Sure. What's up?"

"Maybe I should explain. Alex and Matt come from a pretty traditional Greek family. Their mom and dad really wanted us to have the wedding in the old country."

"In Greece?" Daphne asked.

"Yes. We even started talking about it, but the logistics were insane. Plus, no one in their village speaks much English. Their mom burst into tears when she found out neither of her sons was getting married in Greece. She *ranted*." Her eyes closed halfway as though she were trying to push away the memory.

"What did she say?" Daphne asked.

"I don't know. It was in Greek and Alex refused to translate. But very dramatic."

"I can't wait to meet the mother-in-law of two of my daughters," Daphne said faintly. She sipped her green tea, looking as though she wished it were something stronger.

Marguerite continued, "So, we compromised." She glanced around the table and shook her head. "On a *Greek* wedding held here."

There was a moment of utter silence among a group of women who normally chattered nonstop. Holly said, "A Greek wedding. Here in Oregon?"

"That's right. I can't imagine being married anywhere but on the land where I grew up, where my business is, so in order to stop his mother from crying and carrying on, we had to agree to make it a Greek wedding."

"Greek, how?"

"Well, obviously, Alexei's food trucks will do the catering, and serve authentic Greek food." Lauren thought that was the easy part.

"Okay," Daphne said. "What else?"

"They want the service in Greek and English. She says there's more to Greece than souvlaki and fishermen dancing in a circle."

"Like what?" Daphne wondered aloud. "Boys in flippers dancing to ABBA?" She glanced around. "Seriously, I feel like I'm starring in Mama Mia 3."

Marguerite said, "I should warn you that my soon-to-be mother-in-law is very keen to be involved."

"That's understandable. With the Greek theme," Holly said. "Okay, so we're not quite as far along as we thought. Will I need a translator in order to talk to her?"

Daphne said, "Didn't the Greeks invent farce?" She was looking at Iris, who was a writer as well as a coffee shop owner.

Iris let out a breath. "They certainly invented tragedy."

JOE HAD BEEN DRILLING firefighters for a couple of years now, so figuring out a drill was easy. However, he was used to training professionals, who tended to be fit and pretty knowledgeable about their equipment, whereas here in Hidden Falls, he'd be working with volunteers. He figured he'd treat them like pros and adapt as he needed to. After all, a fire didn't make allowances for who was fighting it.

The following Saturday was dry and clear. Which was excellent. Joe had prepared a backup rainy-day drill for inside the fire station, but he was happy he'd be able to go with plan A: a ladder drill best performed outside.

The Hidden Falls fire chief, like all their firefighters, was a volunteer. Dan Oakley had been a forest ranger in Alaska, taken early retirement, and moved to Hidden Falls. He was strong and fit and had a good head on his shoulders, but the only reason he was chief was because he'd been able to put in more hours of training than any of the other volunteers. Joe had complete respect for people who gave up their free time to help keep their communities safe, but he had to admit that most of these people would never make it as professional firefighters. A lot of them were a little older than he would've liked, and out of shape, but so long as their hearts and wills were there, he knew the Hidden Falls Volunteer Fire Department wasn't about to turn anyone away.

However, more than with fit, professional firefighters, he had to watch out for the health and safety of this group. James arrived early, and, as each volunteer strolled into the big meeting room, he made a point of introducing Joe. An older gentleman walked in, his cheeks ruddy with probable high blood pressure, and, after a quick glance at James, he headed straight to the chairs that had been set up.

James called him back. "Harold, I'd like you to meet Joe Benbow."

Harold had the look of a young prankster who'd just been called to the principal's office as he shuffled forward with his eyes downcast. He stuck out a hand. "Nice to meet you."

Joe shook the proffered hand. "Thanks. You too. Have you been a firefighter for long?"

The older man shook his head. "About a year." And then Harold looked up at James and said, "See you're still walking with a cane. Are you healing all right?"

"Yeah." The word was a gruff single syllable.

The older man nodded and then headed back to where the chairs had been set in three rows, choosing one in the back row.

Joe glanced from one to the other and made an educated guess. "Is that the guy who shot you?"

"Yep. With an antique musket. Tore a chunk out of my ass. I was just lucky the ball didn't hit a little higher. As it is, the physiotherapy is taking longer than we thought. I hope I'll be able to walk by my sister's wedding."

"Your sister's getting married?" He felt like he'd been punched in the chest. Is that why Lauren had been skittish around him? Was she getting married and didn't know how to tell him?

If James heard the intensity in his question, he chose to ignore it. "Yeah. Two of them. Marguerite and Rose. They're marrying Greek brothers, which seems kind of strange, but whatever."

"Huh."

He might've said more, but in that second a new person arrived and his tongue felt as though it had folded over and stuffed itself down his throat. Lauren walked toward him. He'd just been to hell and back thinking she was getting married, then finding out she wasn't. He wasn't ready to see her so soon after the emotional bounce and act like a normal human being.

No one had told him that she was one of the volunteer fire-fighters, but then, it hadn't occurred to him to ask.

James said, "And you know Lauren, of course."

"Yes." He knew he was supposed to ask her something, but he couldn't think what.

In a silence that was just beginning to grow uncomfortable, James said, "Lauren joined the volunteer fire department soon after she moved back here, about six months ago."

Right, that was the question he had meant to ask her. He said, "Thanks for volunteering. It's how communities like Hidden Falls stay safe."

His words sounded formal and stiff to his own ears, and she seemed to be pressing her lips against a smile as she nodded. "I'm really new at this, so I'm looking forward to learning everything I can."

About twenty people filled the room and, with a total force of thirty volunteers, he thought the turnout was pretty good. James introduced him and he looked out at the ragtag bunch of volunteers and knew that come what may, in an emergency they had to pull themselves into a fully operating team. Lives could depend on it.

He said, "I don't live here, but my grandparents do, and on behalf of them and all the other citizens of Hidden Falls, thank you for giving up your time to volunteer for the fire department. Today we're going to work on ladder drills. You all think you know how to use a ladder, but it's one of the most important tools of our trade. There are safe ways to use a ladder and dangerous ones. We're going to learn to use our ladders safely."

A couple of young guys sauntered in late and sat at the back. He figured they were the kind who thought it would be cool to ride in a fire truck and play with fire. They were young and strong, so if they could be properly trained and their attitudes adjusted, they could be excellent volunteers. However, he'd seen enough kids of their stamp that he decided to keep a close eye on them.

He talked first about basic safety, then showed a video. After that, he and Dan demonstrated the correct ways to lift, carry, and position a ladder safely. He had the attention of the volunteers, but he felt they were a little disappointed the he hadn't set fire to something so they could practice with real flames.

"Trust me, it's learning how to use the ladders and hoses, and getting used to working with them while suited up, that will take you to the next level." And then, because they were good sports, and he and Dan had already talked about it, he said, "And next week, using the skills we work on today, we're going to practice on a contained fire."

That perked the volunteers up and they were an enthusiastic bunch who practiced the ladder drill.

Lauren was working with Harold. They had the fire ladder safely propped against the window of the station house and secure. She climbed and Joe was pleased to see that she'd listened to his instructions and was following them. She was nearly at the top when the two young guys who'd come in late paused at the bottom of the ladder and peered up.

"Oh, baby, you can play with my fire hose anytime," one said, and the other giggled.

Lauren stiffened on the ladder but kept going as though she hadn't heard.

But he had. He turned to the two young men and barked, "That is sexual harassment and we have zero tolerance for that behavior here. You'll both drop and give me fifty pushups. Now!"

He rarely used that tone and when he did, he was not disobeyed, not by the men who served with him. But these were volunteers and if they walked away, there wasn't a damn thing he could do about it. Nor would he want to.

For a single second, the kid who'd made the crude remark

wavered. He could see it. But the other kid had already dropped to the ground and was pumping up and down. With a mumbled curse, his buddy dropped and did the same. He counted to fifty out loud, pleased when everybody who didn't have anything more pressing came over to watch.

Nothing like a little peer pressure in the right direction.

When they'd both risen, looking sweaty and foolish, he said, "And now, Bert and Ernie, you can apologize to your fellow fire-fighter."

By this time Lauren was down and her color was as high as that of the kids who'd done fifty pushups. "No," she said, "it's—"

But he stopped her in midsentence. "No," he said. "It's not."

"Sorry," the first kid said, looking down.

"Yeah. Sorry," said the second.

Lauren walked away and he let her go. Then he got the kids working with an older woman who looked ready to put them both over her knee and spank them if they stepped out of line. They'd get a short education in respect today.

James walked by and in a low voice said, "Nice work."

CHAPTER 7

*L*auren wasn't scheduled to visit the Benbow farm, but as she'd finished a call nearby, she called Ernest to suggest she swing by and take out the stitches on the calf. He also wanted her to check another of his heifers to see if she was pregnant. He suspected she was.

As she bumped up the drive, she saw Joe. She gave herself a moment to enjoy the sight of him. He'd really grown into himself, she thought, looking at the tough body and face. Maybe being in a profession where saving lives was part of the job description gave him that look of authority. If she were on the wrong side of a fire, she'd be very glad to know he was in charge of getting her out. It was a nice face, a trustworthy face.

Something had changed since the night they'd worked together getting that calf stitched up. She suspected it might be her own attitude. Seeing Joe with her brothers, especially James, she could tell they'd all put his foolish behavior behind them. Maybe it was time for her to do the same. Joe wasn't bothering her; in fact, he'd given James more attention at the ladder drill. He treated her like a friend.

Apart from her brothers, she'd never had a male friend.

Most of the time, growing up, her brothers were more in the category of tormentors and gross boys than friends. Now that they were older, though, she appreciated them for the men they were. She was close to James, especially, and valued his opinion. She could see the friendship developing between the two men and thought that if James and Joe could be friends, then maybe she and Joe could, too.

She found she liked the idea.

Even as she had that thought, she realized he was acting furtively. He'd been transferring something from the back of his SUV to a backpack. When he saw her, he pushed the backpack into the recesses of the SUV and slammed the back door, then turned to face her with studied nonchalance. In a sketchy guy, she'd wonder if he had the family silver in that pack, but Joe wasn't sketchy.

He waved as she pulled in. When she got out of the truck, he took a step backward as though she emitted a bad smell or something. Sure, her stop before this one had been to check on pigs, but she hadn't been mucking out the sty.

"Nice day," he said.

"It is," she agreed. "I came to take the calf's stitches out. How are they doing after their ordeal in the woods?"

"Pretty well, I think. Grandpa was whistling this morning, so I figure that's as good a sign as any."

She smiled at that. Only someone who knew how taciturn Ernest Benbow was normally could appreciate that for him to be whistling was like a regular person doing backflips across the lawn. "Looks like you've got another pregnancy. Want to walk down with me and see?"

He took a step forward as though he wanted to accompany her, and then halted. "No, that's okay. I've got some stuff to do."

"Okay. I'll see you later then."

She had taken out the stitches and confirmed the pregnancy

before it hit her. Joe had been acting so peculiar because of the *ashes*. It had to be.

It was, as Joe had said, a nice day. Sunny, with only a scattering of clouds off to the west. A perfect day for a hike. Had he been wearing hiking boots? She couldn't remember.

When she asked Ernest about Joe's plans for the day, the man made a rude noise. "Said he had things to do. Ask me, he's slacking. Doesn't want to help rebuild the south fence."

She knew Joe had taken over the morning milking, and every time she was here he was elbow deep in farm chores. For him to take a few hours off was unusual, and yet Ernest was acting as though he was lazy.

And he wondered why he had trouble keeping staff!

When she was finished, she headed back out to her truck. Joe's SUV was gone. She stood, thinking, then walked to the house.

Velma was chopping onions in the kitchen, the radio tuned to the day's news. "Morning, Lauren. Do you want some coffee?"

"No, thanks. I was just wondering if you knew where Joe was." At Velma's surprised look, she added, "I had a question about the fire drill."

"Right, you're one of the volunteer firefighters. Well, don't tell Ernest, but Joe said he needed to get some exercise. You know how important it is for firefighters to stay in shape. He was going to take a quick hike up to Hidden Falls. But he'll be back in time for the five o'clock milking."

"Thank you. I'll catch him later, then."

She got into her truck and debated. She had nothing on her schedule that couldn't be shifted to the next day. If she was right, Joe was scattering his father's ashes, and she didn't want him to have to do it alone. She was already wearing sturdy footwear and she always kept water in her truck. If she'd had more time, she'd have changed into better clothes for a hike, but Hidden

Falls wasn't exactly Everest base camp. Her jeans might be a bit heavy for the climb, but if she wasted time she'd miss Joe.

Clothes didn't matter anyway. Someone should be there to help Joe mark this sad occasion in his life.

Without debating any more, she called in to the vet's office and said she was taking a few hours off. Then she headed for the small parking lot at the bottom of the Hidden Falls trail. And there was Joe's SUV, just as she'd guessed it would be. Since this was a weekday, she wasn't surprised to see that his was the only vehicle parked there.

She pulled up beside it, hoping she was doing the right thing. What if he really wanted to be alone?

Well, when she got there, she'd ask him. If he wanted privacy, she'd leave, but if she were saying good-bye to Jack? Well, apart from the fact that Jack Chance's eventual memorial was going to be crowded with people who knew and loved him, she knew she'd never want to scatter his ashes all alone. If Joe felt differently, all he had to do was tell her.

She grabbed her water bottle and cell phone and started up the trail. If nothing else, the exercise would be good for her. Joe had reminded them that volunteer firefighters were expected to maintain a good level of fitness, and she'd let that part of her life slip a bit lately.

Okay, more than a bit. She discovered that the hill had grown steeper since the last time she'd been up here. She labored and sweated, pushing herself on. She didn't want to pass Joe coming down the trail while she was still toiling upward.

It was beautiful on the trail, though. Nature was turning its mind to spring. She could see new growth coming on the evergreens and even the birds sounded happy the rain had stopped.

As the trail leveled out a bit, she tried to imagine what she'd say when she saw him. *Nice day for a funeral?*

JOE DIDN'T HAVE a lot of happy memories of his dad. But in all fairness, he didn't have a lot of unhappy ones, either. His dad hadn't been around enough.

But the one thing they had done, on one of the rare times they'd been here together to visit Grandma and Grandpa, was hike up to these falls. The few times they'd done it were probably the nicest days they'd ever spent together. His dad had been in a good mood, or he wouldn't have had the energy for the hike. When Frank Benbow was at his best, he was good company, full of optimism and ideas, sure his latest business venture was going to pay off. He'd promised Joe they'd go fishing, that they'd get a house with a real backyard. Of course, it hadn't happened. The deal, like all of his deals, hadn't worked out and there never was a house or a fishing trip. But on the days they'd come up here, they'd had a good time. A father and son time where he could look back and feel good about the memory.

He always thought of his dad when he climbed up to the falls, so it seemed a fitting place to say good-bye.

Joe had always imagined he'd outlive his father, in a hazy kind of way, but not that it would happen so soon. He heard his own heavy breathing like the echo of his thoughts, chastising him. Why hadn't he gone to Bali for a visit? He could have taken some vacation and visited his old man. Maybe he could have helped. Stopped him from drinking so much.

But even as he had the thought, he knew he wouldn't have been able to change Frank Benbow's choices. Frank wasn't a father to be proud of. The last conversation they'd had was about money—his dad asking and Joe refusing.

Maybe he should have wired his old man some cash. If he'd known it would be their last conversation, he might have. As he grew closer, the sound of the falls amplified, pounding like his thoughts. And yet, if he'd sent money, he'd always wonder if the extra cash would have caused Frank to drink so much it triggered the heart attack that killed him.

He couldn't win with his thoughts.

Not today.

Not when the sum total of his father's life was in a coffee can in his backpack. In truth, he hardly noticed the extra weight.

When he emerged into the clearing at the base of the falls, he stopped to catch his breath. There was something cathedral-like about the vast space with the cascade of water tumbling down. He was glad there were no other hikers or picnickers about. He couldn't have completed his task with a group of school kids looking on, or a couple walking their dog. In fact, he'd chosen this time carefully, as the most likely time when he'd have the area to himself.

When Lauren had driven up so unexpectedly, though, just as he'd transferred the ashes to his backpack, he'd felt an impulse to ask her to come along with him. He'd squelched it, knowing she was a busy vet with work to do, and that it was a big request.

She wasn't his girlfriend or even a close friend and yet, apart from his grandparents, she was the only person he'd have wanted to share this moment with.

His father had not been a religious man, but there should be some ceremony to mark his passing from this earth. He unzipped the backpack and eased out the coffee can, which had been easier to transport than the cardboard box he'd received from the crematorium on Bali.

If he'd been thinking, he'd have purchased something on Bali to put his dad's ashes into—a specially carved wooden container ringed by Balinese goddesses, perhaps. But he hadn't been thinking clearly in those hectic days. So, his dad had ridden up to Hidden Falls in an old red Folgers tin he'd found in the tool shed. He didn't suppose Frank would mind, if he was looking down now. He'd probably have yelled down to suggest that his son should have carried him up in a Jack Daniels bottle.

He set the can on a rock in front of the falls and stepped back.

He sat on a big rock for a few minutes, drinking bottled water and thinking about the few times he and his dad had come up here. He hoped, when it was his turn, that he'd leave behind better memories and sadder mourners. He rose and headed toward the tin, glinting as a shaft of sunlight hit it.

He didn't know what made him turn around. It wasn't as though he could hear rustling noises behind him, not with the pounding water in front of him, but some instinct made him turn.

Lauren stood at the head of the trail, where it emerged into the clearing in front of the falls. She looked so beautiful it made his heart ache. Her cheeks were ruddy from the exercise, her hair lay in tendrils around her face, her eyes sparkled, and her chest rose and fell from the exertion.

They looked at each other for a long moment and then she said, "I can go if you want me to. I don't want to intrude, but I thought I'd come along in case you wanted some company."

He was puzzled. "Do you know what I'm doing here?"

She glanced significantly at the coffee can. "Unless you're planning to make an awful lot of coffee, I'm guessing that's your dad in there."

He nodded. Now that she was here, he realized how much he did not want to do this alone. "I'd like you to stay."

She came up beside him and together they pondered the can, splashed by water droplets from the falls. He said, "I brought a poem. Not one I wrote," he added quickly, as a shaft of embarrassment stabbed him at the recollection of the one and only poem he'd ever attempted to write in his life. "Just a poem he read to me when I was a kid."

"You should read it."

He'd only planned to read it silently to himself. He glanced at her. "You mean, aloud?"

"Yes."

He reached into the pack and pulled out the battered, leather-bound book of poetry that had sat in the old glass-fronted bookcase in his grandparents' living room since long before he was born. The book fell open to the page he wanted.

"When my dad would drop me off with my grandparents, he'd read me this poem before he left. I always thought he was trying to explain himself, but maybe he was trying to apologize. I guess I'll never know now, but I can't see or hear it and not think of him. It's Robert Frost."

He knew the poem so well he didn't really need the book, but holding it in his hands reminded him of his father. In his way, his dad had tried his best. He read aloud, not loud enough to be heard over the crash of the water, but loud enough that Lauren could hear him.

> *"Two roads diverged in a yellow wood,*
> *And sorry I could not travel both*
> *And be one traveler, long I stood*
> *And looked down one as far as I could*
> *To where it bent in the undergrowth;*
>
> *"Then took the other, as just as fair,*
> *And having perhaps the better claim,*
> *Because it was grassy and wanted wear;*
> *Though as for that the passing there*
> *Had worn them really about the same,*
>
> *"And both that morning equally lay*
> *In leaves no step had trodden black.*

Oh, I kept the first for another day!
Yet knowing how way leads on to way,
I doubted if I should ever come back.

"I shall be telling this with a sigh
Somewhere ages and ages hence:
Two roads diverged in a wood, and I—
I took the one less traveled by,
And that has made all the difference."

He put the book away carefully, and reached down for the can. He pulled off the lid and, careful not to spill any, in spite of his shaking hands, he scattered the ashes at the foot of the waterfall. The water picked up the ashes and made patterns of them, swirling and tossing them around before carrying them away down the mountain.

He didn't notice Lauren had moved closer until he felt her hand slip into his. She said softly, "Good-bye, Mr. Benbow."

He couldn't speak over the lump in his throat, but silently he said, *Good-bye, Dad.*

As they stood watching, a pale green leaf drifted down and landed on top of the swirling ashes. If Robert Frost were standing here, he'd have made a poem about that.

Lauren's hand felt warm and right in his and they stood there for another minute, watching. He squeezed her hand before letting it go. "Thanks for being here today." He wanted to add how much it meant to him, but he didn't have the right words.

They walked back together, and in spite of his sadness, he felt so much lighter now that his small ceremony was done and the can in his pack was now empty. Somehow it had felt right. His dad would have loved that the prettiest girl in town had come to see him off.

"How did you know? That I was here, I mean?" He still couldn't believe that the one person he'd wanted to be with him had turned up without even being asked.

"I didn't know for sure. But I asked your grandmother where you'd gone and she said you were hiking up here to stay in shape. I figured you'd planned your memorial for today, so I thought I'd see if you wanted company."

"Thanks," he said again. It seemed so inadequate, but he'd made himself a promise that he wouldn't embarrass this woman again. He intended to keep it. She'd shown up and acted like a true friend.

He wanted to keep their friendship more than anything. Because it was better than nothing.

As they walked down, they talked about the fire department and she told him how Marguerite's simple back yard wedding was turning into a Greek-American international incident, with strong-minded mothers on two continents and a translator on call. She made him laugh on a day when he hadn't expected to laugh.

About halfway down she said, "You know, I didn't really know your dad. He wasn't here much, but I do remember one thing. I'd found a raccoon on the side of the road. It had been hit by a car, but not badly. I wasn't sure if I could save it, but I couldn't leave it there, suffering."

"How old were you?" When had she first begun saving lost and damaged creatures?

"About eleven, I think. Anyway, I didn't have a box or anything to put it in, and a wild animal will lash out when it's in pain. I was trying to get it onto a piece of cardboard I'd found in a ditch nearby, when your father pulled over in that cool old car he had. The blue one."

"A 1967 Mustang fastback. That thing was his pride and joy."

"Well, he got out and asked if I was in trouble. I thought that was so nice of him. When he figured out what I was trying to do, he took a box full of cassette tapes that he played in the car, dumped out all the tapes, and using an old towel, we got the raccoon wrapped and in the box. Then he drove me home." She thought for a moment. "I always thought he had a kind heart. Most people around here would have told me to leave it, that raccoons carry rabies and it was going to die anyway. But your dad helped me save it."

In that moment he saw his father caught in an act of random kindness and it meant as much to him as any eulogy. "Thanks," he said. "Thanks for telling me." They rounded a corner and the sun made shadowy leaf patterns on the trail ahead. "Did the raccoon make it?"

"It sure did. Mom wouldn't let me keep it in the house, but Dad let me put it in the barn. Within a week he drove me back to where I'd found it and we let it go. He made me. It was starting to tear his barn apart."

When they reached the trailhead, there were their two vehicles sitting side by side.

He unlocked his, stowed his backpack, and then turned to Lauren. He had no idea what to do. To his surprise, she took one step closer, opened her arms, and gave him a hug.

He pulled her against him and for just a moment, let himself enjoy the feel of her—her warmth, her shape, and the kindness that radiated from her. He pulled away first, even though he wanted to keep her there in his arms forever.

She said, "Would you like to get a beer or something later?"

The shock made his stomach jump. She had a slight blush on her cheeks. He had no doubt she hoped he wouldn't misinterpret her simple act of kindness for anything more. But he knew himself. He couldn't do it. He couldn't hang out with her over a beer, the way he'd do with any other female friend.

If he did, he'd fall for her again.

Making an utter ass of himself once over a woman was bad enough, but twice? It would be all too easy to fall back into unrequited love with this amazing, beautiful woman.

No doubt she was being kind, not wanting him to be alone on the day he'd said good-bye to his dad. Maybe she thought Frank Benbow deserved some kind of a wake, even if it was just two people having an awkward beer.

Even as he knew he had to say no, he couldn't make himself do it.

As though sensing his confusion, she said, "The Roadhouse has live music tonight. Edie usually brings in a band on Tuesday nights."

He couldn't believe it. "Edie? Edie's still running the Roadhouse?" The old woman had been an institution for as long as he could remember. She'd been bartending longer than *anyone* could remember. "I can't believe she hasn't retired."

Lauren smiled and shook her head. "I don't think she'd trust anyone else to run the place, even though she must be nearly eighty. She's like your grandparents. Not ready to give up the work she loves. Anyway, I like to go and support the locals. Mom and Dad might go, and Iris and Geoff if they can get a babysitter. Maybe James and Kim."

Okay, so it wasn't a pity date, or a wake. She was just being neighborly. This was different. They'd be out together in company.

"If Grandpa doesn't have me building fences by moonlight to make up for missing a few hours today, then yes, I'll try to come and join you."

"Great."

He waited while she got into her truck and pulled away, giving him a wave as she turned onto the highway. Then he got into his SUV and drove back to the Benbow farm. As he glanced in his rearview mirror, he could see the backpack containing the empty coffee can.

"You know, Dad," he said, "I could sure use some advice about now. I think I've got girl trouble."

He thought about those two roads in the Robert Frost poem. He had to remember that he'd taken the Lauren Road once before, and that had been a dead end. He was better off on the one less traveled.

CHAPTER 8

"*W*hat's going on? Why do you keep staring at the door?" Paisley asked.

Paisley was a certified genius, and Lauren was happy for her, happy that universities were fighting to give her money and get her into their fancy doctoral programs, happy that she could do the *New York Times* crossword puzzle in less time than it took Lauren to make a cup of coffee, happy that she'd decided to take a year off after her first master's degree and work here in Hidden Falls.

She was much less happy that part of Paisley's skill set was that she was all too observant.

It was a fair question, too. Why *did* she keep staring at the door, willing Joe to walk through it? What was wrong with her? He was a nice guy and they'd shared a special afternoon together. But he was just a friend.

Wasn't he?

She remembered the way she'd felt when they hugged in the parking lot. Maybe she was just feeling a little emotional because they'd said good-bye to Frank Benbow. She'd watched his ashes as they spread out, pushed by the cascading water, and she'd thought about how they would help nurture the land and become part of the life cycle. Something more had happened, though—some shift inside her.

She'd stopped wanting Joe to keep his distance.

When he'd broken the hug and stepped back, she'd been sorry. Maybe that's why she'd invited him to join them at Edie's out of the blue, as though her mouth said words her brain hadn't seen coming.

Edie's Roadhouse had been a cultural landmark in Hidden Falls for longer than any of them had been here. It was dark, old-fashioned, and the wait staff were far from hot, but Edie's was always hopping. Most likely because of Edie herself. She was a small, energetic dynamo of a woman and everybody loved her.

Lauren was with some of her family, crowded around a scarred wooden table. Jack and Daphne, James and Kimberly, and even Iris and Geoff had managed to come out, leaving one of Geoff's former high school students to babysit the twins. By putting her bag on the chair next to her, she'd managed to keep a seat free in case Joe turned up.

Which, so far, he hadn't.

"No reason," she replied in answer to Paisley's question. And then, because she really wanted to talk to someone, she lowered her tone. "Actually, I asked Joe if he wanted to come tonight."

"Joe Benbow?" Paisley looked as surprised as she sounded. "Isn't he the one who serenaded you outside your bedroom window, and sent you bad poetry? I remember I was working on an enriched calculus project that night. I could barely hear myself think with all shrieking and hollering once the boys figured out what was going on." She shook her head, her eyes twinkling in reminiscence. "Not much of a singer, was he?"

"That was almost fifteen years ago. You were just a little kid. I can't believe you remember that."

Paisley shuddered—even her long, reddish-blonde hair shuddered. "Some things you never forget." Then her forehead wrinkled the way it never did when she was working out a difficult math problem, only when much less logical human interactions didn't make sense to her. "Why did you invite him? I thought he embarrassed you so badly you'd never want to see him again."

"Like I said, that was a long time ago and he's changed. He's grown up. He's been helping out at his grandparents' farm, so I've seen a bit of him recently. He's nice." She thought of the way she'd felt in his arms.

Nice didn't come close.

"Does he still have that major crush on you?"

"No." Then she sighed as the truth hit her. "I think maybe I'm the one who has a crush on him."

Paisley nodded. "That's very typical of beautiful girls," she said in the tone of one who has witnessed a lot of beautiful-girl behavior, without ever considering that she might belong to that exclusive club. Paisley, with all her brilliance, never had a clue about how to make the most of her looks, knew nothing about fashion, and cared less. This was a lucky thing since, as the youngest of the Chances, she'd got the worst of the hand-me-downs.

She'd skipped two grades in school. Being so much younger than her cohort, as well as so much smarter, had set her apart. Though she was never bullied by the cool girls, they looked upon her as an oddity and most just ignored her. In her turn, she'd been careful not to get too close to so much exotic beauty in case it bit.

But she had studied the species and she wasn't one to say things idly, so Lauren asked, "What do you mean? What's typical of beautiful girls?"

"I've noticed that exceptionally attractive girls have contempt for the guys who like them. They only want the ones who couldn't care less."

"That is so untrue. And unfair. I've never been like that."

Paisley nodded sagely. "You are a special case. Being the most beautiful woman I've ever seen, you've had too much male attention. Maybe, now that a man is not crushing on you, you have a chance to actually get to know him."

As with most of what Paisley said, this made a lot of sense. "You are very wise for one so young."

Paisley shrugged. "IQ of 148. I can't help it. Any more than you can help being beautiful. These are our burdens and we have to bear them."

Anyone else would have scoffed to hear beauty or brains being looked on as burdensome, but she knew exactly what her younger sister meant. "Do you ever wish you'd been born, you know, not very bright?"

Paisley sipped her beer and took a moment to consider the question. "No. I don't think so. Well, maybe if I were in the *very bright* category, and not *genius*, I would have more choices. I mean, everybody expects me to go to MIT and become a nuclear physicist or something, just because I can, but what if I don't want to? It's like being a really fast runner and everyone expecting you'll head for the Olympics, when you'd rather be a painter. You know?" That clear and all-seeing gaze fixed itself on Lauren's face. "What about you? Do you ever wish you weren't beautiful?"

She'd heard herself referred to as *beautiful* so often that she never bothered to correct people. Instead, she said, "Every single day. I mean, I don't think I'd want to be ugly, but if I could be like Iris or Rose or Marguerite, I'd be so much happier. People say, *She's nice looking and a wonderful baker,* or *She's an excellent doctor,* or *She grows the most amazing organic produce.* But me? No one ever gets past *beautiful.*"

Jack Chance gazed at his two youngest daughters fondly, and put his arm around his wife. In his booming voice, he said, "Look at those two with their heads together. The Beauty and The Brain. What a gifted pair."

Then he looked at Daphne, bewildered. "What did I say? Why are they falling off their chairs laughing?"

At that moment, Edie walked by their table. "How you doing tonight, Jack?" she asked in her raspy voice. "And how'd you get so many pretty girls to sit with you?"

"Edie, when did you get this décor? When Nixon was in diapers?"

She turned to Daphne. "Look at him, with his fancy words. The *décor* is in the washing machine."

While she and Jack traded good-humored insults, Paisley leaned over to Lauren. "Don't look now, but I think your crush just walked in."

She glanced toward the door and sure enough, Joe stood in the entrance. He was casting his gaze over the room and before he saw her, she had a moment to look at him. He wore a gray sweatshirt with the San Diego Fire-Rescue crest on it, and a pair of well-worn jeans and boots. He looked good and she obviously wasn't the only one who thought so. A couple of other women in the roadhouse eyed him up. Then he caught sight of her and raised a hand in greeting.

"Why, that's young Joe Benbow," Jack said. He waved Joe over. "We should ask him to join us."

"Good idea," Paisley said, "Oh, look, there's a chair right beside Lauren."

"Would you shut up?" she said in a low voice to her sister as she pulled her purse off the chair and stashed it.

Joe came over and shook Jack's outstretched hand. "Good to see you back in town," Jack said. "Please, sit and join us. Let us know what you've been up to."

He greeted everyone around the table, was introduced to Kim, and then headed to where Lauren sat.

After kicking her sister's ankle under the table as a warning, she said, "Hi."

"Hi." He settled himself in the seat beside her.

James leaned forward and said, "The guys are still talking about your drill on Saturday. We do the best we can keeping the firefighters in training, but having a professional makes a big difference."

She knew how hard Joe was working on the farm, but he didn't hesitate. "Absolutely. No problem."

"The doctor cleared me for active duty and I don't have to walk with a cane anymore. I want to help wherever I can."

"Great news on all fronts."

Jack said, "I want to join the volunteer firefighters, but the ball and chain won't let me."

Daphne glared. "I'll ball and chain *you* if you ever use that expression with me again. And no, with your heart trouble, I'm not letting you near a fire engine."

"But I want to help."

James looked at his father with fondness. "Just promise not to start any fires, Dad, and we'll consider your civic duty done."

IT WAS obvious that father and son were gearing up for a battle of words, so Iris intervened. "Did you hear that both Marguerite and Rose asked Kimberly to make their wedding cakes?" Iris said to her mom. At least, Joe thought that one was Iris. So many of the Chance girls had flower names it was hard to keep up.

Daphne nodded. "I hope it won't be too much for you," she said to Kimberly.

The shy blonde, who was settled in the circle of James's arm, shook her head, blushing slightly. "No. I like to keep busy." She glanced under her lashes at Hidden Falls' sheriff and the man looked about ready to melt.

A secret message seemed to pass between them and James gave a slight nod. He looked around the table with a grin and said, "I guess Edie's Roadhouse is as good a place as any to make an announcement. Kim and I are getting married, too."

Daphne jumped up and ran around the table to give them both a hug and a smacking kiss on the cheek. "I'm not going to pretend I'm surprised, but I'm so happy for you both. Who'd have believed we'd have another wedding in the family?" Her bright gaze took all of them in.

Personally, Joe figured anyone who'd seen James and Kim together for as long as he had, which was about five minutes, would have figured it out.

"Whatever fool thought it would be a good idea to have eleven kids?" Jack's gruff words were belied by the pride beaming from his face. "It's going to be like *Four Weddings and a Funeral* around here. I just hope we don't have any funerals."

Joe felt his face go stiff. It hadn't been much of a funeral, but he'd said good-bye to his father only a few hours ago. For the second time that day, Lauren slid her hand into his, where it rested on his knee. It was only for a moment, but he felt her warmth and understanding and for that he was grateful.

Daphne whispered something into Jack's ear and the older man looked across the table, his eyes contrite. "Sorry, Joe. I forgot. I'm sorry for your loss."

"Thanks, Jack. It's not like my dad and I were close, but he did his best. It was kind of a shock that he died so young."

Jack nodded. There was a moment of awkward silence and Joe broke it by saying, "I don't know about you people, but I think an engagement calls for a toast." He glanced around. He hadn't been here for a while, but he knew Edie wouldn't be hard to spot. Sure enough, he soon saw her buzzing around, her spiky hair black and tinted with purple at the ends. "Hey, Edie," he yelled over the noise of the bar.

She came over, wearing tight black jeans, boots, and a red sweater covered in sparkles. "Why, if it isn't Joe Benbow. It's good to have you back now you're not trying to sneak in here with an older kid's ID."

He laughed. "Did you have to mention that in front of the sheriff? I can't believe you still remember that."

"Oh, I remember everything that's gone on here over the years." She chuckled. "Wait till I write my memoirs. There's going to be some red faces."

"Or you could take up blackmail, and get rich."

"I'm rich enough. Teasing you people is my reward. What can I get you?"

"The sheriff here just got engaged. We'd like a bottle of your finest French champagne."

The older woman looked over at the newly engaged couple. "Congratulations, James and Kimberly. You two look so young I always think I should card you, but when you get to my age, everybody looks like a kid. I hope you'll be very happy." Then she turned back to Joe and put a hand on her hip. "And if I were running a wine bar, like they do in *San Diego*, I might stock French champagne."

He leaned back, enjoying himself. "What have you got that's good for a celebration?"

"I'll go have a look in my *wine cellar* and get my *wine steward* to send something out."

"Thanks, Edie. And put it on my tab."

He didn't know where she dug it out from, but within a few minutes a bottle of sparkling California wine appeared, along with wine glasses. The Roadhouse, Edie informed them with satisfaction, didn't run to champagne flutes. It was still a merry and joyous celebration.

Jack looked at him as Edie poured the wine. "Well, son, as the provider of this fine champagne, you should make the toast to the happy couple."

It wasn't what he'd planned, but if he could head a team of firefighters all risking their lives, he figured he could manage a speech. To Edie, he said, "Pour one for yourself." And Jack nodded approval.

They all looked at him in expectation as he stood and raised his glass. He felt Lauren's gaze on him, along with everyone else's, and he wanted to say something true about love and commitment.

"Kim, I don't know you very well—in fact, we only met a few minutes ago—but I've tasted some of your baking and I think anyone who can cook like that must have a sweetness inside them."

"Oh, she does," Daphne said.

"And James, here, I've known a lot longer. Be glad you didn't know him then. He was a little rough around the edges, like when he and his brothers threw me in the family pond and damned near drowned me."

"It was the only way to stop the caterwauling when you were singing that godawful love song to my sister," James exclaimed. They were all laughing around the table, even Lauren. He'd never have believed he could see the humor in his teenage humiliation, but looking back from the man he was now to the boy he was then, he could see what a ridiculous figure he must have been, and laugh at his younger self.

That moment had marked him forever. He'd seen people transformed after a fire destroyed their homes and all their possessions, but so long as their loved ones survived, he was amazed at how resilient people were, how they started fresh.

That night had been his turning point—the moment he'd grown up from a romantic boy who'd believed all he had to do was want a woman badly enough, prove himself worthy enough, and she'd fall into his arms, to a man who understood that he had to grow into himself before any woman would want him.

They'd all grown up since then, including James. He said to Kimberly, "You wouldn't have looked at him twice then."

"True," Iris said, laughing.

"But he's grown up. Now he's the guy who tries to keep this town safe. He's proven himself. When I see the way you two look at each other—" Suddenly, Grandma's words came back to him from so long ago. "I can see that it's right. You two fit. And so, we raise our glasses to your future happiness. Kim and Jim forever!"

"Kim and Jim forever," everyone chorused, raising their glasses and drinking.

James turned to him, mock serious. "You ever call me Jim again, you'll go back in that pond."

"Not without all your brothers helping you, *and* your dad."

Kimberly reached over and touched his hand. "That was a beautiful speech. Thank you."

"It was," Lauren said quietly beside him.

"Well, I got work to do. Congrats, you two. And don't ever move away. One of you keeps us safe and one feeds our sweet tooth. You're almost as important around here as the one who provides the beer." Edie glanced under her fake lashes at Joe. "And champagne."

"Are you getting married in our backyard, too?" Jack wanted to know after Edie hustled off.

James shook his head. "We're getting married in Canada. In a place called Nelson, where Kim's family are from. You're all welcome to come."

Joe felt a tension run around the table that he didn't understand and then Jack, who could always be counted on to say the thing no one wanted to say, scratched his head. "But I thought Kim's old man was a—um, not someone you wanted to spend much time with?" He looked to James, who seemed to tighten his arm around Kimberly, who'd hung her head. Then he said, "Ow!" and turned to his wife. "What?"

James said, "It's okay. Now that marijuana is legal in Canada, Kim's dad has turned legit. He opened a store."

Wow. A former drug dealer or grower or whatever Kim's dad was into didn't seem like someone James would be thrilled to call Dad, but Joe knew better than anyone that you didn't get to choose the person you fell in love with. "So now you can meet him."

"Now I can see where Kim grew up and meet all her family. Plus, it's supposed be beautiful there."

"At least now I only have two weddings to worry about. Of course, Marguerite is going to be married on our property. Rose has been down looking at big hotels and country clubs in the area. I thought she'd get married in Portland, but she's decided she wants to be married here, close to home, so more of her friends can attend." Daphne looked at Kimberly. "I hope Rose isn't asking for too complicated a cake. I imagined she'd go to one of those celebrity bakers."

Even though Joe didn't know her well, Kimberly was clearly glowing with happiness. She said, "You know, it's funny. Marguerite and Rose have similar ideas about what they want. I'll have fun putting their different personalities into each cake."

Jack said, "I'm building a gazebo for Marguerite's wedding."

The Chance brothers and sisters all shared a look of alarm. Lauren said, "Does Marguerite know about this?"

"No. And don't tell her. It's a surprise. I got this great idea from Pinterest, where you build a gazebo and then hang candles from it. It will be beautiful in the evening."

"Couldn't they just have a tent, like every other wedding?" James wanted to know.

"Marguerite doesn't like the tent idea. She said so. She'll love my gazebo, because she's got imagination, unlike some of my kids."

James tried to argue his father out of the gazebo idea, and Joe felt a little sorry for Jack. Beneath the noise he leaned over and said quietly to Lauren, "Why are they busting his chops over this? Seems like he really wants to do it." He wasn't sure what Pinterest even was, but Jack seemed excited.

"Remember, the gazebo is a surprise," Jack said. "I don't want anyone telling Marguerite."

"Won't she see it when she's home? If it's big enough to get married under, I'm guessing it's not that small," James said.

"I'll hide it when she's home. In the barn beside the chicken coop."

Paisley and Lauren exchanged a glance before Lauren answered Joe's question. "Dad loves to build things. But he's not very good at it. We're just worried that in the middle of the wedding the gazebo will fall on the happy couple."

"Oh." He got a mental image of the mayhem. "That would be bad."

"Exactly. So now, in order to prevent disaster, the night before the wedding, Prescott and James will have to sneak out and make sure the gazebo's sound. They'll probably have to rebuild it and hope Dad doesn't notice, because no one ever wants to hurt his feelings." She looked over at her father, who was trying to find the Pinterest photo on his phone so he could show it to James. "He never had a childhood or a family, and now he wants to give us everything. It means so much to him to make these things, and he does it with all his heart. How can we not at least pretend to be happy?"

He'd have to discover when the wedding was. Because if he

was still here, Joe thought he'd like to help make sure the gazebo was secure. And help figure out a way to do it quietly so Jack would never know. "You're lucky to have a father like that."

"I know. He's the best." There was something about this family that made a person feel at home, part of the clan; except there was nothing brotherly about his feelings for Lauren. Just sitting beside her was torture. When she moved, she occasionally brushed against him, and he could smell the citrusy scent of her shampoo in her hair, feel the warmth of her body so close to his.

He had no choice but to try very hard not to do anything that would ruin this budding friendship.

He was man enough now to know that Lauren was way out of his league and a friendship was all he could have. Well, as hard as it would be, he'd take it. When she'd shown up today at the falls for his impromptu farewell ceremony for his father, he'd experienced her kindness. When she wasn't nervous that she'd get hit on, she was interesting to talk to, warm and funny. She'd be a loyal friend, and those weren't so easy to find. Sure, he'd love to have more, but friendship wasn't bad.

Edie soon had a full house. At nine, she turned off the piped-in music, climbed onto the stage, and announced the singer who'd come all the way from Tacoma to entertain them tonight. The man who settled himself on the stage with a guitar looked as though he'd spent too many nights in places like this. He was probably in his late thirties, worn around the edges, with a world-weary air. He had nice voice, though, and Joe sat back to listen.

The singer looked around the Roadhouse as he finished his first set, and Joe felt the moment his gaze landed on Lauren. He stumbled over the final line of the song.

He felt her stiffen beside him. She tried to pretend she hadn't noticed, but of course she had. After that, the poor guy couldn't take his eyes off her. Joe felt her unease and wished the bozo with the guitar could find something else to look at. The fact that he understood the poor sap's dilemma didn't irritate him any less.

Halfway through the second set, the singer said, "I haven't sung this song in a while, but tonight, I'm going to give it a try. It's by Alan Jackson. It's called *I'm in Love with You Baby and I Don't Know Your Name.*"

Paisley snorted with laughter. James glanced over at him and said, "At least this one doesn't make dogs howl and windows break."

It was so obvious the doofus up on stage was singing to Lauren. He didn't even try to hide it. He might as well have been under a magic spell. It was also obvious to Joe, at least, that when the set was over the guy would be wandering over here to try to make time. He wondered how to head the guy off at the pass, not only for his sake, but for Lauren's.

But while he was trying to think of things that might actually help, Lauren was gathering her things together. "I've got an early morning at work. I think I'm going to head out now."

Of course she had a lot more experience at warding off the lovelorn than he had. He rose at the same time. "Good idea. Ernest will have my head if I'm not up by five for the milking."

He leaned over to James and Kimberly and said, "Congratulations again. I'll see you at the firehouse on Saturday." Then he followed Lauren. He was tempted to loop his arm around her in a proprietary fashion, but she might misinterpret the gesture and knee him in the balls.

Instead, he made do with a nod to the singer that he hoped combined two messages: *Thanks for the music.*

And *Oh, by the way? The lady is with me.*

When they were out in the relative quiet of the parking lot, he said, "That singer couldn't take his eyes off you."

She didn't say anything, but she didn't have to. Then, "Some days I wish I was already old."

In Joe's opinion, she was going to be beautiful forever. He bet she'd still be fighting off old goats in the seniors home. "Don't wish your life away. Life is short enough as it is."

"I know. And he didn't mean any harm," she said.

"But he made you uncomfortable, and that's what makes me mad." He paused. Then he confessed, "Well, what really makes me mad is that I used to be one of those guys. I hope you can forgive me. I was young, and stupid, and I've learned my lesson."

In the moonlight her eyes were luminous. More goddess than woman. Lord help him, he had it as bad as that poor besotted singer. But at least he now understood that he was firmly in the friend zone. And he was determined to be okay with that.

So, he walked her to her truck, opened the door for her in spite of her protests, and waited until she pulled out before getting into his own vehicle. There'd been a moment, just a moment, when he'd been standing there with the door open and she'd come up close to him. In a different time, with a different woman, he'd have leaned over and kissed her.

It took every bit of his self-control not to obey that instinct. Not to taste those plump pink lips.

Lauren deserved better. She deserved a man who could be a good friend without making a fool of himself over her. It wouldn't be easy, but he was determined to be that man.

And who knew? Maybe, once she'd accepted and trusted him as a friend, she'd start to see him as potentially more.

He scoffed at his own foolishness as he drove the lonely road to his grandparents' place and his old bedroom that always made him feel like a teenager again.

Maybe he'd wake up in the morning and find the cows had milked themselves.

CHAPTER 9

$\mathcal{L}$auren was asleep when the call came. Comfy in bed, she had her phone set to *Do Not Disturb*, since she wasn't the on-call after-hours vet this week. That meant that only emergency calls could get through. That included two people: her mom and the fire dispatch operator.

She grabbed her blaring phone and checked the time. It was four a.m. and her adrenalin immediately started to do its job. She was wide awake, her feet already on the floor when she picked up and heard the details of the emergency she was being called out for.

As a volunteer firefighter, she didn't have to respond to calls. The chief was firm that they should put their families first, then their paying jobs. But this was a real fire and she'd never refuse if one of her neighbors was in danger. She got the address and then felt her heart pound into overdrive. *"Where* did you say it is?"

The dispatcher repeated the address. "It's the Chance place."

Normally, they met at the station to get suited up and take last-minute instructions, but her home was closer. "Tell the chief I'll meet them there."

There was no way she was going to waste time heading for the fire department and suiting up. Not if her family was in danger.

She put on sturdy boots and a bright yellow rain jacket so she'd be visible, grabbed a spare pair of gloves, then ran for her truck. She floored the gas pedal, and as she turned into the lane leading to her parents' place, she heard, faintly but distinctly, the sound of the fire engine on its way. In the back of her mind she registered admiration and pride that they'd got the engine out so soon.

The house appeared to be fine—no flames, no smoke, nobody standing outside in nightwear looking stunned and frightened. But then she pulled around to the side and saw her mom in jeans and a robe, hauling a garden hose. When she looked beyond her mom, she saw the smoke.

It was coming from the barn. Jack had an ax and looked as though he was going in. "The gazebo," he yelled.

"Mom, fire department's on its way. Don't let Dad go in there."

Her mom turned and said, "Jack, no. Don't even think about it." She left her mom to deal with Dad, knowing she'd keep him safe.

She didn't give a flying fig about the gazebo. What had her sprinting forward was the ominous stream of smoke coming from the attached henhouse.

As she'd learned in her training, fire could hide inside a building, getting stronger, working its way through vulnerable old timbers, before suddenly springing visibly to life. She'd also learned in her training never to go in alone. But she knew every one of those chickens. Most of them were rescues, birds too old to lay anymore that had been abandoned, lost birds, and the ones that needed rehoming. She thought of the two little white Silkies, Snow and Flake, who came running when they heard her voice, knowing she always brought treats. And the Rhode Island Red who'd been fending for herself in the wild when someone found the bird and brought it to Daphne. Auntie Mame had been skinny and frightened, half her feathers missing. Now, she was plump and happy.

Lauren couldn't stand the thought of them trapped inside a burning coop. And they were trapped. They were free-range birds, so had the run of a fenced yard during the day, but at night they roosted in the coop, the door shut against predators.

She put on her gloves and then opened the door. The birds were panicked, too frightened to run for the door and freedom. She glanced around and while the smoke was ominous, there were no flames. Knowing she was going against all the rules, she pulled her T-shirt up over her mouth and nose and went in.

The siren grew louder. The fire engine must have arrived. Good.

She grabbed two of the birds running in circles at her feet, ran outside with them, and went back in. There was lots of time. Fortunately, the fire was on the other side of a thick wooden wall.

She was soothing Elsie, a Speckled Sussex, who'd pushed her head right under Lauren's arm and into her armpit in terror, and heading for the door, shooing a few more birds toward the opening, when she heard a noise behind her like an explosion.

No, she thought dimly, not *like* an explosion. It *was* an explosion.

She ran for the door, but the blast had shaken everything and part of the roof caved in, blocking her exit.

Don't panic, she said to herself even as everything inside her wanted to do just that. The fire department was here on the property. They'd get to her. But of course, they'd gone to the other side of the barn, where the source of the fire was. By the time anyone realized there was somebody in the attached chicken coop, it might be too late. A lot more people died of smoke inhalation than burned to death.

She heard voices, now, the sound of an ax. She went to the door—or what was left of it. And, through the small opening, yelled, "Help!"

Then she began to push the chickens through the opening. *Please let someone notice them and realize where I am.*

JOE WAS proud of the volunteers. They were following protocol, acting like a team. They'd been turned out and on site within five minutes of the call coming in. He was surprised that Lauren wasn't among them, considering it was her family home, but he didn't have time to give her more than a moment's thought.

They had an actual fire to put out, and, since it was in a barn rather than a home with people inside, it was an excellent practice ground. Naturally, since he wasn't the chief, he didn't give the orders, only took them.

"Let's get some lighting here," Dan ordered. "Where's the water source?"

Joe told him about the pond, where he'd been dumped all those years before. At least the knowledge now came in handy. It would be easier and closer than getting a pumping hose down the well. He made sure the hose got unpacked properly, and directed the guys manning the hose to the pond.

Daphne came running up to him. "Get Jack away from there, will you? He's not strong enough for this. Not with his heart. Lauren told him to stay back, but he wouldn't listen."

"Lauren's here?" He hadn't seen her. Alarm began to beat in his chest. "Where is she?" Would she have gone into the house for some reason?

Daphne looked around, confused. "She was here, right before you guys got here."

And then he heard Lauren's cry for help. If he hadn't been so hyperalert, he doubted he'd have heard her over the yelling of men, the sound of an ax splitting wood, the rumble of the engine.

But he did hear her.

Abandoning Daphne, he ran toward where the voice had come from. The outside lights came on and he saw chickens running around, dazed and panicked.

Of course she'd gone for the animals. But where was she? "Lauren," he yelled. "Where are you?"

"In here. In the hen house." She coughed. "Door fell in. We're trapped."

"I'm coming," he yelled.

He ran back to the fire truck, got an ax, and called to the chief, "Dan, Lauren's trapped in the chicken coop." He didn't wait for instructions; he sprinted back to the attached structure. He found the door under the partly collapsed roof but he didn't like the look of it. If he went at it with an ax, the whole thing might cave in. "Lauren, I'm coming in from the side. Stay back."

"Okay." She sounded a lot calmer than he felt. He recalled their conversation at the Roadhouse about Jack's terrible building skills. What if he'd built that chicken coop?

He'd never wielded an ax with such force or speed. He felt as though all his fear and his need to save Lauren were channeled into his muscles. He struck all the way through the crappy structure on his first swing. His biggest fear was that the entire structure would topple onto her, so he tried to make the opening small enough for her to crawl through, hoping he was staying away from any supporting beams.

Sweat broke out all over his body. Hadn't the chief heard

him? All the activity was on the other side. He got the opening big enough, he hoped, then put his head inside.

There she was—crouching on the other side, her shirt over her nose and mouth, two hens under her arms.

She wasn't even wearing her suit! He twisted his body and got in even as she stumbled forward, eyes streaming from the smoke.

"I've got you," he said, as he had so many times in the past. Usually he'd said the words to complete strangers. "I've got you." He put his arm around her and guided her to the opening. She pushed a chicken into his gloved hands before climbing out.

He tucked the hen under his arm the way she had, and then he pulled her away from the building into a clear patch of dirt and grass. She fell to her knees, coughing, and he fell to his in front of her. Both chickens wriggled their way free and jumped down. Now that the adrenalin was easing, his muscles didn't seem to be working. He was panting with the effort.

"Thank you," she said, gasping. "I got all the chickens out."

She was okay. Not hurt. Fine, in fact. And she was worried about a bunch of chickens? He was filled with irrational fury.

"How could you have been so stupid?" he shouted. "You could have died in there. For a few birds? Are you crazy?"

She looked stunned as he kept shouting, right in her face. Her eyes were big and red-rimmed, and when he gripped her arms, he could feel her shaking. Or maybe that was him.

"But I know those birds. I couldn't let them die."

And suddenly all the fight went out of him and he pulled her to him, kissing her. Kissing her as though he'd never stop.

She tasted of smoke, and sweetness, and he wanted to hold her in his arms and keep her safe forever. He was vaguely aware that the hoses were now pumping, and the birds were fussing all around them.

Then she pulled away, and coughed.

He heard a crack and turned his head to see the roof of the chicken coop fall in. Five more minutes and he would have been too late.

~

"I CAN'T BELIEVE Joe made them bring me to the hospital," Lauren complained. "And now they send you?"

Rose Chance glared at her sister through narrowed eyes. "Just be glad they didn't have to send the coroner. What were you thinking, running into a burning building after those chickens?"

"I was thinking of the chickens, because I'm a veterinarian," she snapped. "And the building wasn't burning at the time. I got trapped when the other one exploded." She saw the way Rose was looking at her, her eyebrows raised, and shook her head. "No, Dad didn't build that barn. It was already on the property when they moved in."

"It was still a rickety old barn, whoever built it."

"I know. That'll teach me." She coughed again. "So, am I permanently damaged?"

Rose shook her head. "The smoke irritated your bronchial tubes. You'll cough for a few hours, but you'll be fine."

"Then why did they send me all the way to Portland for you? Not that I'm not happy to see you, Dr. Sister."

"Relax. I was planning to come this weekend anyway to do some wedding planning." She shook her head. "I thought Dad would end up here, too. He's so upset about what happened."

"But it wasn't his fault."

"Actually, it was. Seems he's been building a special gazebo with built-in candleholders. He tried it out in the barn and he must have left one of the candles still lit when he left for the night."

"Oh, poor Dad. He wanted to surprise Marguerite."

"He surprised everybody." To Lauren's shock, she burst out laughing, and Lauren joined in. Her chuckles hurt her throat, but she was relieved that she hadn't done any permanent damage.

Except maybe to her relationship with Joe. She'd never forget the way he'd yelled at her, the raw fury in his tone, and then she had yelled back, and then... it had changed to something as hot and dangerous as the flames consuming the barn. When he'd pulled her in and kissed her, her world had slid sideways.

She'd have kissed him forever, if a coughing fit hadn't overtaken her. Then he'd pulled away as though she'd slapped him, and next thing she knew, she was being bundled up and taken to hospital. By her brother.

She hadn't seen Joe since.

CHAPTER 10

*L*auren found Joe at the Benbow farm, chopping wood. Since they heated their home partly by wood stove, there was always chopping and stacking to be done. He had his back to her and was stripped down to the waist. It was a beautiful sight to watch those muscles at play, the way his biceps bulged, the bunch and stretch in his shoulders and back. A shiver of memory went through her as she recalled the feel of his mouth on hers, hot and angry.

The way he was attacking the wood, it looked like he was still angry.

She'd have liked to stand here and watch him chop wood for an hour or two, but she'd come to apologize and she wanted the words said so she could get over this nervous feeling in her stomach. For two days she'd waited to hear from him, hoping he'd check that she was okay, since he was the one who'd high-handedly demanded she be taken to hospital.

He hadn't even driven her there himself. He'd told Dan to arrange it, as though he were the chief. Naturally, Dan had agreed. Dan was so impressed that they had a professional fire-fighter in town that he'd do anything Joe said. It was James who had driven her to the hospital in the end. Daphne was busy looking after her husband, who'd looked gray and sick as he watched the barn burn.

James had received the call, too, and while he probably agreed with Joe that she'd been a fool to run into danger without her turnouts, on account of a flock of birds, he didn't criticize her. He was her big brother, telling her he'd have her at the hospital in no time and completely ignoring her arguments that she didn't need medical attention.

Joe hadn't called her the day after to make sure she was okay. He phoned Daphne to check that she hadn't sustained any harm. He hadn't called the woman he'd pulled from danger and kissed senseless, he'd phoned her mother!

He must still be angry. She might have ignored him as studiously as he was ignoring her, except for the little fact that he had saved her, possibly from death, and he'd been right to yell at her. What she'd done was stupid. She'd not only put herself in danger, but Joe as well.

If other firefighters had had to break into that burning barn to rescue her, she'd have endangered them, too. Just the sight of Joe with an ax in his hand took her back to those moments of being trapped inside the henhouse, hearing the sound of the ax breaking wood, praying he'd get her out before the roof fell in or the walls burst into flame.

Somehow, even though he'd been wearing turnouts, she'd known it was Joe. Known it was him wielding the ax with such cool determination. And when she saw him, she'd experienced a wave of relief. She'd be okay. Joe wouldn't let anything happen to her.

He split another log and then paused to wipe sweat from his forehead. Since he was wearing work gloves, he had to use his forearm. It was possibly the single sexiest sight she'd ever witnessed.

In the sudden silence, she said, "Joe?"

For a frozen moment he stood there as though he hadn't heard her. Then slowly he turned, his face carefully wiped of all expression. "Hey."

He didn't look all that happy to see her. In fact, he looked as though he didn't want to see her at all.

What on earth? If she'd felt nervous before, she felt even worse now, looking at his masklike face. "Hi. I wanted to talk to you." Well, that was obvious. Great start. He didn't reply, so she hurried on. "I owe you an apology. As a firefighter, I'm aware that what I did was dangerous."

"And stupid," he added.

"Right. Stupid and dangerous. And I wanted to thank you for saving me."

There was a beat of silence. He leaned the head of the ax against the toe of his boot. "I'm a firefighter. It's what I'm trained to do."

His eyes were cool, businesslike.

Right, so she was just a job. Another life saved in the long list of people Joe Benbow had pulled from burning buildings and barns. People trapped in cars and cats in trees. She was no more important to him than Fifi caught in the apple tree.

Saving the chickens had been what she was trained to do. They'd all survived the trauma, but she didn't think she'd share that.

"Well, anyway, thank you."

"You're welcome," he said, without even cracking a smile.

"I hear Marguerite invited you to her wedding, since you saved her maid of honor."

He nodded. "Rose, too."

Okay, that surprised her. "That's a lot of Chance weddings." No doubt James would also put him on the list, since the two of them had become such pals, bonding over the safety of Hidden Falls and its citizens.

"I'm not sure I'll be able to go." He began swinging the ax gently, back and forth. "I've got to head back soon. I've got a real job, a life."

As though this one weren't real.

Now it made sense, the huge pile of freshly chopped wood beside him. He was laying in a store of firewood to last the months until he could come back. Doing what he could for his grandparents until the next time he got leave. She supposed, given the length of time he'd already been away from work, that it would be a while.

As though he'd read her mind, he said, "Not sure when I'll be able to come up here again."

And that kiss? Had it meant nothing to him?

Maybe it was because she'd been oxygen deprived and grateful to be alive that she'd felt as though that kiss had made her life change course. Everything until that instant was one part of her life, and then he'd rocked her world, and now she was in a new phase. But he acted as though the kiss hadn't even happened.

Could it have been a hallucination?

But even as she had the thought, she dismissed it. For one thing, her imagination wasn't that good. For another, he was acting different, too. Not *I kissed you and you rocked my world* different. More like, *I kissed you in the actual, literal heat of the moment and I regret it so let's tacitly agree it never happened.*

She could never forget that kiss, but she owed him a lot, so if he wanted to pretend it hadn't happened, she could give him that.

"Well, I hope you'll say good-bye before you go." It was all she could think to say.

"Yes. Of course."

"Okay, then. I'll get moving. Got a lot to do today."

But before she could get in her truck and drive away, Velma opened the back door. "Lauren, come into the house for a moment. I need to see for myself that you're all right." Here was the genuine concern. Here was the kind of response a person usually expected when they'd nearly died. "Do you have time for coffee?"

Oh, she definitely would like some coffee to go with that sympathy. Not that her parents weren't full of sympathy, but since her dad felt like he'd nearly murdered one of his beloved children, and her mom was worried about how hard her dad was taking the fire, the sympathy was on the painful side.

Sitting in Velma's kitchen, with fresh coffee and an extra-large slice of apple cake, she began to feel better.

"You were so brave," Velma said—the first and only person to see that, even if she'd been foolish, her motives had been good. "Did you get all the chickens to safety?"

"Yes. They're all fine. A little freaked out, and of course, they don't like sleeping in used dog crates, but when we get the new henhouse built, they'll be back to normal. She hesitated and then said, "Joe pulled me to safety, you know."

Velma sipped her own coffee. "When that boy got home, all covered in soot and with that haunted look in his eyes, I thought someone had died."

Really? "No. He saved me. Singlehandedly."

"He's been like a bear with a sore head ever since. I don't know what's got into him."

Patch woke from where he'd been napping in the corner of the kitchen and trotted over for a pat. "Maybe he feels guilty that he has to leave you and Ernest."

"We'll miss him, of course. But he has his own life to live." The older woman's eyes clouded with sorrow. "If Frank had wanted to be a dairy farmer, maybe things would have been different. Joe would have grown into it. But he's happy with his life." She glanced at Lauren. "I think."

Lauren accepted a second cup of coffee, hoping that Joe might join them. He had to know she was still here—her truck was parked out in front. When she heard the door, she felt herself blush. But it was Ernest who came in, saying in his gruff way, "I'm awful glad to see you safe, little lady."

He patted her on the shoulder. For Ernest, the gesture equated to a heartfelt hug. "I'm glad I'm safe, too. I was telling Velma that it was Joe who pulled me out."

He gave a curt nod, but she could see he was pleased. "Didn't know that. Boy doesn't boast, I'm glad to say."

Then talk turned, as it always did with Ernest, to the herd. "Three new calves came along yesterday," he said. "Brings the herd to two hundred and twelve."

"That's great." Since she hadn't been called, the births had to have been trouble free. "Do you want me to take a look at them?"

"No need. They're in good shape."

"Wonderful."

She couldn't stay much longer without making it obvious she was waiting to see Joe. And Joe was just as obviously staying outside until she left. She didn't want him to strain something chopping wood too long, so she rose, gave Patch a final pat and said, "I'll be on my way, then."

"Where's Joe?" Ernest said. "He said he had to go into town. I thought he'd be in by now and showering."

"Just leave it be," his wife said in her calm way.

As Lauren stepped outside, she had to accept that Joe did not want to see her.

Turning out of the Benbow farm, she didn't know what to do or where to go. It was the same feeling she'd experienced once when she went into an exam prepared for communicable diseases among farm animals and, in fact, the exam had been about internal diseases of domestic pets. She'd been unprepared, baffled, and slightly panicked.

That's how she'd felt during her conversation with Joe. She drove her truck to the end of the drive and then hesitated before turning left in the direction of the Chance family home.

As she bumped down the road leading to her parents' house, she told herself that she was only here to check on the chickens. The reality was that she needed someone to talk to who might understand what she was going through. Naturally, she did check on the chickens, who were scratching and pecking and having dust baths as though nothing untoward had happened.

Their behaviors all appeared perfectly normal. At the sound of her voice, they ran up to her, knowing she'd have treats. She fed them corn and bird seed, watching their antics with a smile. Auntie Mame sat on her lap in the sun and the rest was good for both of them. Half an hour among the birds left her much calmer. No wonder she'd become a vet; animals were so much easier to understand than human beings.

Before she went into the house, she peeked into the barn and shuddered. The inside of the barn was blackened and the remains of the gazebo looked like a giant, charred skeleton. But worse was the attached chicken coop. Already, someone had started tearing down what was left of it. She thought of the minutes she'd spent trapped inside and the way Joe had come for her, like a hero.

How ironic that he'd attempted to win her with bad singing and even worse poetry and she'd wanted nothing to do with him. Then, years later, he acted like a true hero and she wanted him badly, but now he wanted nothing to do with her.

As she turned and walked toward the house, she wondered how any two people ever got over themselves enough to fall in love.

She found her mother and three sisters all sitting around the big dining table working on Marguerite's wedding. There were samples of fabric, and a dozen bridal magazines all spiky with colored Post-It Notes, and two vases of various flowers, from simple daisies to roses and hydrangeas. She wished she'd phoned ahead to find out what they were doing, because all the happiness of two soon-to-be-married sisters and one young mother was enough to make a girl a bit envious. Paisley was in the adjoining living room with her nose in a book, as usual, her legs pulled up under her, idly twirling one of her curls around her index finger. She thought at first that at least her younger sister had escaped Wedding Central, but it turned out that Marguerite had asked her to read a poem at the wedding and she was searching out suitable verses.

Lauren glanced over Paisley's shoulder and wrinkled her nose. "'The Rime of the Ancient Mariner'? Do you think that's a very good poem to read at a wedding?"

Paisley looked up with the vague expression she often wore when she'd been pulled out of a book. Lauren watched as she replayed the question in her head and then she shifted, as though making herself more comfortable in the corner of the sofa. "I got carried away. You know how reading one poem leads you into the next poem, and you forget what you were looking for?"

She plopped herself down beside Paisley, reaching over to pat her on the head with affection. "You are such a geek."

Marguerite glanced up from the bridal magazine she was flipping through. "I know I saw the rustic table idea in this magazine. I think." Then she focused on Lauren. "Are you really feeling okay, Lauren? You look a little pale."

No doubt her sister was referring to nearly getting killed in a fire, but the real shock she'd suffered was finding that Joe didn't even want to talk to her. "No. I feel fine. I mean, Yes, I feel fine."

"Okay, so long as you feel fine."

Daphne came in from the kitchen at that moment and headed straight over to Lauren. "But you did have a terrible ordeal. And Marguerite's right—you look very pale." She turned to Rose, who was making notes in an expensive leather-bound notebook. She was probably the only doctor on the planet who had impeccably neat handwriting. "Rose, are you sure the doctors checked out Lauren thoroughly?"

"Yes, Mom. And I went over the tests myself. She's right— she's fine."

"She doesn't look fine."

Marguerite said, "Do you think you'll be well enough to go shopping for a bridesmaid's dress this weekend?"

Rose glanced up again. "Wait a minute. I want you to be my bridesmaid. I want all my sisters."

Lauren sighed. "I don't suppose I could wear the same bridesmaid dress twice? Your wedding guests will be different people than Marguerite's."

"No, they won't. For a start, we'll both have the same in-laws and their families, and of course I'm going to invite all our friends from Hidden Falls."

"Really? I thought you'd have all these stuffy rich people at your wedding."

"If you mean Prescott, our brother can't help himself. He was born stuffy. And Evan's not very rich now that he's not a corporate shark anymore, just a regular small-town lawyer."

Marguerite laughed. "You know I didn't mean our brothers. I meant your fancy Portland friends."

Rose looked around at all of them, and as she raised her hands, her gigantic diamond engagement ring twinkled. "I want my wedding to be about family and close friends. And most of them are still here. Plus, there are quite a few of the Vasilopolous clan coming."

"Huh. I thought your wedding would be a lot more fancy."

"No. That's my honeymoon. We're flying to this remote resort in the Cook Islands. It has a Michelin-starred chef and it's rated seven stars."

"That's a lot of stars."

"The honeymoon's about me and Matt, but the wedding, that's about family."

Lauren felt confused. "But you've been touring all these expensive venues."

"Only because Marguerite is already getting married here, at the house, and two weddings at the house might be too much." She looked almost guilty as she said, "And I don't want to wait until next year to get married. Matt and I want to start a family by then."

Daphne and Iris shared a glance and Marguerite and Rose shared a glance. Lauren would have shared a glance with Paisley if her nose hadn't been back in the poetry book. Finally, Daphne said, "I'm seeing an easy solution here, girls."

Marguerite nodded enthusiastically. "Absolutely. Why don't we have a double wedding?" She pulled up the vision board that she'd been adding to as pictures and ideas and swatches of fabric caught her fancy. "It's going to be casual, but nice, and you could add in your own ideas about decor and so on."

Rose pulled the vision board toward her. On it was a picture of Alexei's food truck. "Is Alex catering his own wedding?"

"Of course not. His staff are going to do it, using his recipes. But if you wanted to have a different kind of food, I'm sure we could make it work."

Rose began to look quite enthusiastic. "No! I really wanted to have Alexei cater our wedding. I mean, how perfect for the Greek people to eat genuine Greek food cooked by the groom and his staff. Even our soon-to-be mother-in-law wouldn't dare complain about the food if Alex cooked it." The two brides high-fived each other. "Matt and I didn't want to ask him, because, obviously, he has his own wedding to plan."

Daphne said, "How many people are we talking here? With guests and families?"

The two brides began going over their separate lists of guests and it was amazing how similar they were. Marguerite had a few more organic farmers and yogis on her list, and Rose had a few fellow MDs, but there was plenty of room on the Chance property. And, as their mom pointed out, they could always rent a bigger tent.

"What about that Greek tragedy of a mother?"

Rose said, "I think she'd be really happy. Then the relatives from the old country only have to travel here once. And so do the parents."

"I think we should let Holly know, if anyone can make this work it's her."

"And she can add another service to her website. She planned "My Big Fat Greek *Double* Wedding.""

Marguerite said, "I feel so bad that Dad was building us a gazebo and now it's ruined."

"Just be glad you weren't standing under it when it caught fire," the more practical Rose commented.

"Oh, I see you invited Joe Benbow." Marguerite was going over Rose's list. "I was going to invite him, too." They both glanced at Lauren and, at the same time, said, "Is he coming?"

The awkward scene from this morning was still fresh in her mind. She said irritably, "Why are you asking me? How would I know?"

Rose and Marguerite both put down their guest lists. Daphne set down the vision board. Iris turned from her sleeping babies. Lucky, the family's golden retriever, chose that moment to wander over and put her head in Lauren's lap, and even Paisley put down her book to stare at her next oldest sister.

It was Iris who spoke. "Because the air sizzles when you two are together."

She shook her head, wondering how all the women in her family could be so completely wrong about something so simple. "I thought we were friends, but today when I tried to apologize for, you know, putting his life in danger over the chickens, he was completely cold with me. He's definitely not interested."

Rose said, "I'm a little out of the loop, but isn't Joe Benbow the one who's been in love with you since he was, like, sixteen years old?"

"Yep," said Marguerite.

"And, isn't he the one who wrote that terrible poetry and, even worse, composed a love song and sang it outside of our window?"

"Yep," said Marguerite. "Guys have been crushing on Lauren since she was old enough to have hormones, but I've never seen anyone who had it as bad as Joe Benbow did."

"He's the one the boys finally dumped in the pond, right?"

Daphne chuckled and said, "That was very unkind of them, but that poor boy would not stop singing."

Lauren said, "Well, he seems to have recovered from his teenaged crush."

"Not from where I was sitting, at the Roadhouse," Daphne said.

"Trust me, he wants nothing more to do with me." She felt sick inside, and she really didn't want to talk about this any more. Naturally, her mother and sisters completely ignored her delicate hint to shut up already.

"I don't get it. What's going on?" Iris asked.

It was Paisley who answered. "Lauren's never been rejected before. Never. Not once, in her whole life. Boys, young men, old men, and a few women have made fools of themselves over her, and been rejected, but it's never happened to her."

Rose nodded. "Oh my gosh—as usual, Paisley's correct. Anyone you ever wanted you could've had with a snap of your fingers. But with Joe, you've hit a speed bump, and you don't know how to handle it. You actually have zero experience with rejection."

And, frankly, she would've been quite happy to keep that record unbroken. "Well, I have now, and you don't have to look so happy about it."

Rose's lips tilted in a smile that looked borderline evil. "You can't blame us mere mortals for being just a little bit happy."

Iris said, "Something happened between the Roadhouse and this morning. More than the fire. What aren't you telling us?" Iris was like Hidden Falls' unpaid therapist. Everyone went to her with their problems, and she'd been listening to those of her brothers and sisters for most of her life. It was like her to try and get to the bottom of the problem so that she could solve it.

And, because Lauren really did want to understand what was going on, and these were the women she was closest to in all the world, she said, "I think it was the kiss."

CHAPTER 11

"*E*xcuse me? Can we back up a little bit here?" Marguerite said. "What kiss? When?"

"How was it?" added Daphne.

"It was right after he pulled me out of the henhouse. He'd broken in through the side wall with an ax. I was never so glad to see anybody in my life, and then he pulled me out to safety, and when we both had our breath back, he started yelling at me."

"Whoa whoa whoa. What's all this about yelling?" Daphne demanded. "I thought you said there was kissing?"

"Well, first there was yelling. He really let me have it, telling me I was irresponsible and stupid to risk my life for a bunch of chickens."

"He had a point," Rose said.

"I save animals like you save people. It's what I do. But he was so mad, like, over-the-top angry. And I was coughing, and trying to explain, and then in the middle of it all, he suddenly grabbed me and kissed me."

Iris and Daphne both nodded, as though there were some kind of secret code and they'd just cracked it.

"Ah, angry kissing," Iris said. "Geoff did that to me when he found me on top of the step ladder hanging a baby mobile at about eight months pregnant. First he got me down, then he yelled, and then he kissed me so hard, I could feel him shaking, and he made me promise I would never do anything so stupid again. It's because he was afraid of losing me. Because he loves me."

"I think Joe was shaking too, when he kissed me," Lauren admitted.

"I don't think he wants to be just friends." Iris said the words, but all the women nodded as though they agreed with her.

Lauren was so frustrated she wanted to pull her hair out. "It doesn't matter. He's leaving anyway. As he reminded me this morning, his life isn't here. It's in San Diego."

"Right, that pesky thing called his career seems to be getting in the way of true love," Rose said.

"It's too bad he can't stay," Daphne said. "His grandparents could really use his help. At least, if he was seeing you, he'd come home more often. And you could go down there and visit when you had holidays, or fly down for a weekend."

It wasn't an ideal situation, but a long-distance relationship would still be better than this misery. "So, what do I do?"

One of the babies woke and started to fuss. Iris picked Liam up, settled herself in one of the big, comfy chairs in the living room, and began to nurse him. There was a moment of intense silence as they collectively held their breath, hoping Mia, the other twin, would remain sleeping for long enough that her brother could complete his meal before she started on hers. Lauren had no idea how Iris managed it, but somehow she kept both kids fed and healthy.

Once Iris was settled, she responded to the question still hanging in the air. "What do you want to do? What do you want to happen with you and Joe?"

What did she want? She'd always put so much effort into worrying about the men who so foolishly fell for her, that she rarely thought about what she wanted. Any dates she had were almost so she wouldn't have to hurt a man's feelings by turning him down, and because she'd always found the easiest way to turn a man down gently was to let him know she already had a boyfriend.

But Joe was different. He wasn't begging her to go out with him—quite the opposite. He seemed determined to keep his distance.

Now, when she thought about it, she knew what she wanted. "I don't want a long-distance relationship. I want him to stay."

"What if he can't?" Rose asked. "Would you relocate?"

"You mean, follow him?"

"You might want to ask him first. You know, whether he wants you to."

Marguerite suddenly snorted with laughter. "I'm sorry, but look at her face. Our Lauren has never chased a boy before. I guess there's a first time for everything. But it's kind of charming."

She did not feel charmed, or charming. She felt sick to her stomach. They hadn't been there this morning when Joe was so cold to her, so dismissive. But what if they were right?

"Okay, assuming you're right and he kissed me—he angry-kissed me—because he cares—" The general nodding suggested they did assume they were right. "Then why was he so weird with me this morning?"

Paisley rested her book on her knee, clearly more interested in Lauren's botched love life than wedding poetry. "He did make a super huge fool of himself over you when you were teenagers. Maybe he's still embarrassed."

"But that was years ago."

Paisley, who read books the way other people ate candy bars, said, "You should have been born in the Middle Ages."

"What?" Her sister might be a genius, but sometimes she said the strangest things.

"Courtly love. It was a thing, in the Middle Ages. A knight would see a beautiful woman and then he'd immediately run out and slay dragons for her, or do brave and impossible deeds, all to win the love of a woman he'd never even spoken to. That's what you're like. You're that woman. And Joe wrote you poetry and sang that terrible song he wrote and instead of winning your love, he got chucked in the pond." She looked around at them all. "If it had been the fourteen hundreds, he could have jousted for your favor, which I think he would have been better at. You're just way out of your time."

Lauren resisted the urge to laugh, since Paisley was clearly serious. "Well, since I don't have a time machine handy, maybe we could work with what we have."

"I think Paisley might be right," Daphne said. And when they all stared, she went on, "Not just about courtly love, but the other thing. I've raised plenty of boys and the ego of a teenaged boy is both huge and fragile. Maybe he's too afraid to be hurt again."

"I also think we need to consider the possibility that he's over Lauren," Rose offered. "He's grown out of her."

"Grown out of me? Like I'm an old T-shirt that got too small?" She did not like this theory. She did not like it at all. Her sisters and her mother all seemed to think it was a perfectly reasonable possibility, from the way they were nodding, putting their heads to one side or, in the case of Iris, looking sympathetic.

They didn't know that she had followed Joe up the trail and taken part in his impromptu good-bye ceremony for his father. Joe hadn't pushed her away then, but he hadn't really encouraged her either. What was he going to do? Tell her she couldn't be on a public trail? She'd thought he had genuinely appreciated her sharing that moment with him. And she remembered the way his hand had felt in hers. The way their palms had pressed against each other. The silent communication. Had she been the only one who felt anything?

Then she closed her eyes against the realization that *she* was the one who had put her hand into *his*. What was the poor guy supposed to do? She'd taken his hand again, at the Roadhouse, to which *she* had invited *him*. No wonder he was leaving soon.

She was acting like a stalker.

Paisley closed her book of poetry with a sigh and set it on a side table. Sounding like a twenty-two-year-old university lecturer, which she could have been if she'd wanted to, she said, "We now have two competing theories to consider. The first is that Joe Benbow is still crazy about Lauren, but acting distant to protect his ego. Have I got that right?"

Daphne nodded. "Yes. And my proof is the angry kissing and the way he was acting at the Roadhouse." She looked at Lauren. "You left the Roadhouse together. Did he make any sort of move on you?"

She thought of the way she had hesitated well within kissing distance and he had not taken her up on her unspoken invitation. Well, teenaged boys were not the only ones with fragile egos. She decided not to share that. Instead, she said, "He held the door of my truck open for me while I climbed in, and then waited until I was driving away before he got into his own vehicle."

"That shows very good manners. I bet that's his grandparents' influence," Daphne said.

"Doesn't do much for the theory that he's still crazy about her, though," Rose said, clearly still preferring her own suggestion.

Paisley continued, "The second theory is that he's just not into you."

Lauren did not like this theory at all. She much preferred the first one.

Rose said, "The only proof is that he's not doing anything to pursue Lauren or to see if she likes him better now that he's a hot firefighter than when he was a skinny, emotionally immature teenager."

They all looked at Paisley. She was the genius. If anyone could figure out which of these two theories was correct, presumably it would be her. She creased her brow and looked off into the distance, the way she did when wrestling with a particularly thorny physics problem, but after a moment she shook her head. "It's impossible to tell. There are too many variables, too many unknowns. We need more evidence."

"Evidence? What is this, a murder investigation? I just want to know if a guy likes me or not."

Marguerite said, "You could always try the daisy game." When they all looked at her she made a plucking motion with her fingers. "You know—he loves me, he loves me not."

"I think I want something more concrete."

But Marguerite was already reaching for the vase on the table, pulling the daisies out and handing each woman a flower. Lauren took hers with foreboding. A droplet of water from the bright green stem plopped on her jeans. "Why is everyone getting a daisy?"

"Because it's not a game if it's just you doing it."

She looked at all of them, each with a daisy in hand. "So how does it work? The most yeses or nos wins? Best out of five?"

"You're as bad as Paisley. Just pull the petals already."

She took a deep breath. "This is silly." But her heart was pounding as she grasped a yellow petal and pulled. "He loves me." The yellow petal fluttered to the ground, to be followed by a second. "He loves me not." A few more petals swirled before she said, "I never knew a daisy had so many petals."

"These are Marguerite daisies," her mother informed her. "That's why I chose them."

She was down to two petals when she noticed that none of the other women had pulled a single one. All of them were looking at her, as though the answer to her love life could be found in a daisy. "He loves me."

A single petal remained. She fought a foolish urge to cry as she reached for the last petal.

"It's just a silly flower," Daphne said. "It doesn't mean anything." But she sounded upset.

Gently, she pulled the last petal from the flower, as though it were the last of her hopes. "He loves me not." Then, as she stared at the denuded center, she saw something. "Wait! There's a baby petal. It was hiding under the others." She waved the flower stem with the midget yellow petal clinging to the round part in the center that Marguerite would know the name of and which she neither knew nor cared.

"There is!" said Daphne, who suddenly seemed to believe in the power of the daisy.

"He loves me!" she cried.

Rose pushed her unmolested daisy back into the vase. "Why don't you ask Joe to be your date to the wedding?"

"We don't even know if he'll be here."

"Well, if he likes you, he'll fly back for the weekend."

They all looked to Paisley, who nodded. "I think that would give us the proof we need. If he's willing to fly back to be your date, he definitely likes you. If he makes an excuse, you probably need to move on." Paisley looked at the confetti of daisy petals at her feet and then at Marguerite. "No offense to the daisy fortune teller."

Lauren couldn't believe this idea. It was the worst she had

ever heard in her life. "You're telling me I should ask a guy out on a date?" She could hear the horror in her own words.

"I can't believe it," Iris said. "You made it to twenty-eight years old and you've never experienced unrequited love?"

"No. I haven't. I have to tell you, it sucks."

As though in agreement, little Mia woke up and began to cry.

CHAPTER 12

*J*oe chopped wood until his arms were begging for relief, and his back felt like he'd been run over by a stampeding bull. But there was something satisfying about the sound of the ax breaking into the wood, and the growing pile of winter fuel for his grandparents.

He was leaving soon and he felt terrible abandoning them like this. But what could he do?

And why did Lauren have to come around looking so heartbreakingly beautiful, reminding him of what he could never have?

If only he hadn't kissed her, he could've gone on with that tenuous pretense at friendship. But now that he'd felt her against him, felt her lips trembling beneath his, he knew they could never be friends. He'd been fooling himself thinking they could.

Chopping wood was a constant reminder of those terrible minutes when he'd known that she was stuck inside an unstable building, made of old, dry wood, the most flammable of organic substances. He never again wanted to experience anything like the emotions that had gripped him.

He'd fought like a madman to break through and reach her. When he thought of all the ways that could have gone wrong, like some of the tragedies he'd witnessed in his years as a fire-fighter, he knew how lucky she had been. Still, his fury had been all out of proportion. He knew it was reaction, and hoped she understood that.

But the kissing? There'd been no excuse for that.

He'd stepped way over the line he'd drawn for himself, and now that he'd experienced what it felt like to hold her in his arms, he knew he could never be merely her friend.

There was something about Lauren—and it wasn't just her beauty—that made a man want it all. He wanted to keep her safe, cherish her, make her happy. And all she wanted was to be friends. It was hopeless.

Unrequited love could ruin your whole day.

He stacked the firewood and then indulged in a long, hot shower before heading into town to pick up a new head gasket for one of the tractors. When he returned home, he passed a shiny Lincoln pulling out of his grandparents' drive.

He grabbed the gasket, deciding he'd do the job tomorrow morning after milking, and then walked up to the house wondering what his grandmother had planned for supper. Smelled like lasagna, he thought, as he entered the house.

Patch was the only one who greeted him when he came in. No cheery hello from Grandma, or a question about the price barked from Grandpa. He stood the gasket in the mudroom and found his grandparents sitting in their accustomed seats at the kitchen table and the identical expressions on their faces made him blurt, "Did somebody die?" At their age, they were starting to lose old friends and colleagues.

His grandmother attempted a smile and shook her head. "No. How was your trip into town?"

Only then did he notice a business card sitting on the table between them. It must belong to the person driving that Lincoln. He read the card and his stomach plunged. "A real estate agent? Why was there a Realtor here?"

"It was that nice Bonnie Pennington. She stops in to see us every few months. She sure loves my apple cake."

He glanced from one to the other. "You know that apple cake isn't what she really wants, right? She's hoping you'll put your property on the market, and she'll get the listing."

"She's a businesswoman," Ernest said with a shrug. "She's got bills to pay same as anybody else. She's just trying to make a living. I respect that."

Velma nodded. "We've both agreed that she'll get the listing when we decide to sell."

Heat crept up the back of his neck and circled his ears. If a real estate agent was coming by regularly, she wasn't doing it out of the goodness of her heart. She must sense she had a hot prospect here. He'd always known that his grandparents couldn't continue to run the farm forever, but were they seriously thinking about selling up? Without telling him?

"Are you thinking of selling anytime soon?" He tried to keep his tone neutral, but even he could hear the curt way the words emerged from his mouth.

Suddenly, Ernest stood to his full, lanky, six foot one and glared. "What would you have us do? I'll be eighty next spring and your grandmother's not far behind me. You think we can keep on getting up at dawn, milking, worrying about the price of milk or the health of the herd and paying taxes and maintaining this place? How long do you think we can keep doing it?"

He sounded angry, but Joe knew it was frustration driving him. He felt an answering frustration echo inside himself.

"We hoped your father would grow up and become a farmer." Grief creased Grandpa's face for a moment and then he carried on, as stern as always. "But obviously that didn't happen.

And then we pinned our hopes on you. But we can hear you on the phone, talking to your fire chief, telling him you'll be back soon."

He felt helpless and guilty. "It's my job. What I'm trained for. I want to help here as much as I can, and if things were different—"

For one crazy second he pictured himself and Lauren in one of those hazy montages common to television commercials and Hallmark movies. He and Lauren, working the farm together, his grandparents sitting on matching porch rockers watching over them. His vision even included a cradle on the front porch, beside his grandmother.

Pitiful, impossible dreams.

"We know that," Grandpa said. "You've made your own life, and, given your beginnings, you've done a damn fine job of it. I don't say this to you much—don't want you getting a swelled head—but your grandmother and I are proud of you. Deeply proud. But we've got to be sensible. If we sell soon, while the herd's healthy and the land's looking good, and the books show a profitable organization, we can get a decent price. Hopefully enough to last us until we croak. If we wait too long... Well, we don't want to wait too long."

He thought he could hear Realtor-speak in the phrases his grandfather was using, but she wasn't telling them anything but the truth. He felt torn. The reality was, he'd put down a few roots in San Diego, but they weren't deep. He didn't have a wife or family of his own; he could sell his townhouse and walk away with few regrets. He'd miss some of the guys he worked with, but they'd stay in touch.

He could move up here and run the farm with Grandpa's help—and probably keep hired help more easily. But did he really want to be a dairy farmer? And what was a farmer without a farmer's wife?

"Look, promise me one thing. You won't do anything hasty, and you won't let Bonnie whatever-her-name-is slap a For Sale sign on this property without talking to me first."

Grandpa looked as though he was about to send him out to do more chores for talking back. "You think we don't know our own business? You think we need some young buck like you to make sure we don't get cheated?"

Once, that look would have had him quivering in his boots, but he was all grown up now. He pulled himself to his own six foot one and glared right back. "I think you know your own business fine. I also think you know that I love you and Grandma. And yes, I want to make sure you don't get cheated. You have a problem with that?"

He could have laughed at the expression on his grandfather's face. Almost.

Grandpa wasn't a man who expressed his love in words. He was more given to rough pats on the shoulder and the odd grudging word of praise. Having his grandson tell him to his face that he loved him caused him to look proud, embarrassed, and irked all at the same time.

After a moment he said, "No. I don't suppose we do."

"Good."

His grandmother stood and opened the oven door, releasing the delicious smell of the bubbling lasagna. "Well, if you two have finished your peeing contest, let's eat."

He had to laugh, and to his surprise his grandpa joined in. Grandma moved the business card to the counter beside the old landline they still used. And all through their meal he thought of it there, like an unwelcome fourth at dinner.

~

JOE WAS HELPING his granddad fix a stretch of broken fence. They hadn't discussed the possibility of his grandparents' selling the property any further, but he supposed they had a tacit understanding that the list of jobs they were trying to get through before he left were all things that would improve the appeal of the farm to a potential buyer. He bet Bonnie the Realtor had penned them a nice little list of jobs, like fixing this stretch of fence, and repainting the front hall, which no one ever used because everybody in town came through the back door.

However, he understood that it was a lot harder for his grandparents to think about moving than it was for him to think about them selling up and going, so he kept his thoughts to himself. The worst part was that selling the farm would be a terrible mistake. It was their home and a business that had sustained their family for half a century.

The thought of another family here made him feel sick.

At first, he thought he was feeling nothing but guilt, but as he worked, he began to accept that what he felt was *possessive*. This wasn't his farm, obviously, but one day it should be. That's what his grandparents would want. Not enough money to buy a condo and retire. The thought of Grandpa cooped up in a condo made him smile. It was never going to happen.

This was home. And not only for them, he realized, as he banged nails and painted walls. It was the only real home he'd ever known. They'd as good as brought him up, and if it hadn't been for them, he had no idea what would have happened to him.

How had he never understood that before? When he was out there at five in the morning, he was part of the rhythm of the farm. When he helped birth a calf or rebuilt a tractor engine, even when he chopped firewood, he was part of this farm and he was only now seeing—when it was nearly gone—that it was part of him.

He was losing sleep, torn between *should I go?* and *should I stay?*

He was a trained firefighter. He had a job he liked, colleagues he respected.

And he was a farmer. Like it or not. The gene must have skipped a generation.

His cell phone rang. He didn't recognize the number so he answered, "Joe Benbow."

"Hello, Joe. This is Daphne Chance." Of all the people he might have imagined on the other end of that call, he'd never have guessed it would be Lauren's mother.

"Daphne, hi." Ernest raised his eyebrows when he overheard, and Joe shrugged, letting the nosy old guy know that he had no idea why she was calling.

She didn't keep him waiting long. "I'm giving an engagement dinner for James and Kimberly on Saturday, I wondered if you'd like to come? James thinks so highly of you, and he's so grateful for all the help you've given him in the fire department. Plus, you were there when they announced they were getting married, and also, we're so grateful to you for all your help with that fire." Then she laughed, a very girlish, giggly sound for a woman of her age. "I've given you a lot of reasons to come, but of course, if you're busy, I'll understand."

She'd given him a lot of reasons, but the one that was causing warning bells to sound in his head louder than a five-alarm fire was that Lauren would be there. Did she even know that her mom was inviting him? Daphne obviously misinterpreted his silence, for she said, "James only agreed to this dinner if I made it absolutely clear that there are to be no gifts. We're just having a celebration with friends."

Now she made him feel like a cheapskate, when he hadn't even thought about gifts; he'd been too busy wondering whether he could attend the same party as Lauren without making a fool of himself.

Again.

Well, fool or not, he liked James, and he liked the Chance family... now that they'd grown up. "Sure. I'd love to come. Thanks."

"That's wonderful. We'll see you Saturday, any time after five."

While he and Grandpa finished replacing a rotted fence post, he filled in any details his grandpa might not have overheard, which wasn't for lack of straining his ears.

When he was done, Ernest said, "James, that's the sheriff."

"Yep." His grandpa knew perfectly well who James Chance was.

"Lauren the vet's brother."

"Yep," he said again.

Grandpa looked at him from under bushy gray brows, his blue eyes piercing. "That's a very pretty girl."

"Yep," he said for a third time. "Pass me the post-hole digger."

Grandpa did. "You make sure and wear something nice on Saturday night."

"You did *what?*" Lauren asked her mother, which wasn't that easy with her mouth hanging open in shock and horror.

"I invited Joe Benbow to James and Kimberly's engagement party. I thought you'd be pleased."

She narrowed her eyes. "No, you didn't. If you thought I'd be pleased, you might have checked with me first." She was so mortified she considered coming down with some convenient flu bug on Saturday night. He was going to think she'd asked her mother to invite him.

"Don't be silly, darling. The least we can do is serve him dinner, after he saved your life."

She didn't answer. The obvious response—that it was her father who had put her life in danger in the first place—didn't seem appropriate. After a moment, her mother carried on. "Anyway, he said he'd be delighted to come."

"Well, you'd better have some other single girls at the party. I'm serious. What if he thinks this is a setup? Which, knowing you, it probably is."

"Lauren Elizabeth Chance. When in your life have you ever needed to be set up? Of course he won't think that."

"Well, I'm inviting my good friend Kirstin Backhouse."

"You can't invite her. She and James used to date each other."

"I think she knows that James is seeing someone else, and she is still single."

On a break between calls, she stopped in at Sunflower for a coffee and one of Iris's Morning Glory muffins. She poured out her frustration at their mother's matchmaking efforts and begged both Iris and Kimberly to add some more single women to the guest list. She didn't even bother trying to hide what was going on from Kimberly, since she already thought of her as another sister.

The bride-to-be blushed. "I'm so sorry to cause all this trouble. I thought it was so nice of your mother to throw an engagement party, but I'd be really unhappy if it caused you any embarrassment."

Iris turned to her. "Would you stop being so polite and Canadian? You're going to be one of us soon—you have to toughen up, girl. Mom loves you, and she wants to put on a party for you and James. Embarrassing Lauren is just a bonus."

"Very funny," Lauren said. "And Kim, she's right. This is your special night. I don't want to be a buzz kill, but please, can you invite a couple of single girlfriends?"

"Sure, but then we have to invite a couple more single guys as well, or it will be weird."

Iris put in, "I'll talk to Cooper. He can invite some of his friends." At the expression on Lauren's face, she said, "Not the sculptor. I'll make him promise not to invite the sculptor."

Kim's eyes widened. "What's wrong with the sculptor?"

"Let's just say that now we know what Lauren looks like in marble. Naked."

CHAPTER 13

*J*oe arrived at the fire station a half hour early on Saturday, to get things ready for today's drill. Since it was raining, he decided to go for hose work that they could do inside. They'd had their real fire practice at the Chance place, but he'd noticed a bit of fumbling with the hose —at least, he'd noticed it once Lauren had been packed off to the hospital and he could think straight.

He was pretty sure that the firefighters would all want to work on hoses since they'd so recently experienced how important it was to get it right. While he was setting things up, James came strolling in. He said, "I thought that was your vehicle parked outside. You have a second?"

"Sure." He couldn't imagine what James would want to talk to him about badly enough to pull off the highway and into the fire station just because he'd seen Joe's SUV. They were seeing each other later at the Chance place.

Nobody was around, but James walked to the corner of the training room anyway. "You know that all the police, fire, and emergency services come under my budget, right?"

"I hadn't really thought about it, but sure."

"We keep our fire department going through fundraising. Community fairs like our Fall Fair and the Fourth of July, which usually only make money and don't cause havoc." He paused and absentmindedly rubbed his left hip. "But that only pays for equipment and suits. For manpower, we've got some amazing volunteers, as you've seen, but I think it would be great if we had at least one professional firefighter to work with us on a permanent basis."

Joe nodded, but didn't say anything. He waited for James to continue. The sheriff said, "I've got some extra money in my budget for another deputy. But we don't really need another deputy; we need someone with firefighting experience. Someone like you."

Joe let his surprise show. "Are you offering me a job?"

James nodded. "You're probably making more money where you are, but yes, I am. I've talked this over with the mayor, and he agrees with me. We have to post the position, obviously, but I wanted to talk to you first. See if you have any interest."

"Wow. I sure didn't see this coming." He thought about how much it would mean to his grandparents if he could stay, how they wouldn't have to sell the farm, because he'd live there and be able to help them. Sure, the money would be less, but so would his living expenses. There was plenty of room on his grandparents' property for a second house. They could build something smaller, at first for him, and then maybe for Velma and Ernest when the big house got to be too much.

This was everything he wanted, tied up in a pretty bow. Well, almost everything he wanted. And he had no idea if he had it in him to face rejection again. "Can I think about it?"

"Absolutely. I'll drop you an email with all the details, the benefits package, and so on. Call me anytime if you want to discuss it. You know, you fit right in here. We'd love to have you back."

"Thanks. One more thing. Can you not mention this to anyone?" He did not want his decision to be influenced by well-meaning citizens of Hidden Falls who might try to make up his mind for him.

"Understood. Nobody knows about this but me and the mayor, and he'll keep his mouth shut if I ask him to."

"Send me that email. I'll think about it seriously."

They shook hands. James said, "I'll see you tonight." He took a step away and then turned back. "I hope my mom didn't force you to come. She gets very enthusiastic when she likes someone." Then he grinned. "You save one of her kids from a fire, and you're going to be invited to everything from her Sunday family dinners to every wedding, baby shower, and vegan potluck."

"Vegan potluck?"

"It's a thing. You move here and you'll find yourself some night eating a plate of salad and nuts and talking about auras. Don't say I didn't warn you." He walked off laughing.

Lauren didn't come to the drill. She sent her regrets with another volunteer, said she had been called out on a veterinary emergency.

No doubt it was true, and he was relieved not to have to see her when she stirred up so many painful memories and impossible dreams. But, of course, he missed her like crazy. He might actually have it worse now than he had at sixteen.

WHEN GRANDPA HAD TOLD him to make sure and dress nicely for James and Kimberly's engagement party, he'd probably imagined a suit-and-tie sort of outfit, being that he was old school. Joe contented himself with wearing his best jeans, the dark blue shirt his last girlfriend had helped him pick out at a trendy place in LA, and the only pair of dress shoes he'd brought with him. He had no tie, but he'd thrown in a sports jacket when he was packing, just in case. When he arrived at the Chance place a little after six, the engagement party was already in full swing. He hadn't been sure what to expect, whether it was going to be just the family, or a bigger do, but there had to be fifty people milling around indoors and spilling outdoors, thanks to a spell of warm weather.

Kimberly stood in the doorway to the living room and reminded him of a Christmas card angel, with her blue dress and shining fair hair. She was surrounded by a small group of women who were *ooh*ing and *ahh*ing over the engagement ring he could just see sparkling on her hand. He steered his way around them, looking for someone to talk to—preferably another single guy.

As his gaze swept over the group on the back lawn, he spotted Jack Chance who, from the way his voice was booming and his arms were swinging, was telling some tall tale. Clearly, he had recovered from the trauma of the fire he'd started.

Daphne came rushing up to him, in a loose-fitting purple dress. "Oh, Joe," she said, then stopped. "Gosh, that rhymes! I'm so glad you could come. Do you know anyone here at all? Well, the boys of course, and I'm sure you'll recognize some of your old friends."

"Great. Nice party."

She said, "Lauren had an emergency, but she should be here soon."

Was he that transparent? Could she tell he'd been looking for Lauren? "That's okay. I know a few people. Thanks."

Daphne then introduced him to a young woman wearing a tight black dress and a lot of silver jewelry. "Kirstin Backhouse. She's a friend of Lauren's. She only moved here a couple of years ago."

"Hi," he said.

Kirstin was the drama teacher at Jefferson High, she told him. "I teach with Geoff, Iris's husband. I used to date James. Before Kimberly, obviously. But if you live in Hidden Falls long enough, you're bound to date a Chance some time."

He laughed and thought, *If only*. She said, "So, have you?"

"Dated a Chance? No." Nearly died of hopeless teenaged love for one? Oh, yeah.

"Well, you'd better hurry up. They're getting snapped up like cookies." He wondered if she'd been drinking, then saw the way she looked at James, who was in a group of single guys, and thought maybe he wasn't the only one suffering from unrequited love.

She waved a hand around the room and he imagined she'd come from an acting background before teaching drama. She spoke with such precision and the gesture would have worked well on stage. As it was, she nearly knocked the beer out of his hand. "Iris has Geoff. Marguerite and Rose are both engaged. Paisley's too young for you. Probably also too smart. And then there's Lauren."

"What about Lauren?"

"Oh, my God. You're not another victim, are you? Lauren is that girl every woman wants to be and every guy wants to have. Who could compete with that? She'll end up marrying a celebrity or a billionaire or something. If one of them ever comes to Hidden Falls."

"She seems pretty happy as a vet."

Kirstin shook her head. "I've spent some time on Broadway. She's that girl all the musicals are about. The one in the small town who gets discovered." She took a sip of her drink. "We're friends. Because she's even nice, like that girl in the Broadway musicals. Everybody likes Lauren, but she's obviously destined for greater things."

At that moment, the woman who was destined for greater things walked in.

She wore a shapeless beige dress, had her hair in a braid down her back, and dress boots on her feet. She could not have done less to enhance her looks.

Kirstin said pretty much what he was thinking. "How can any woman put so little effort into her appearance and still outshine every other female in the room? If I wasn't a better person, I'd hate her."

She must have seen both of them looking at her, for Lauren hesitated and then came toward them. "Kirstin, Joe, hi. How's the party?"

"Great," said Kirstin. He just mumbled something noncommittal and wished he were a celebrity or a billionaire. Preferably a celebrity billionaire, so all bases were covered and he could sweep her off her feet and into his arms. He could tell that Lauren was about to move away when Kirstin beat her to it.

She said, "I'm going to congratulate James on his engagement." And she walked away. Joe now saw that James was momentarily alone in the garden.

Lauren watched her go and said, "They used to date."

"Yes. She told me."

They both watched through the window, as though it were a TV screen—Kirstin walking up, talking to James, running her hands through her hair. If she'd been acting *I miss you and I wish you weren't getting married,* they'd get it in the third balcony.

"I thought she was over him," Lauren said.

"I don't think so." He felt sorry for Kirstin, a fellow sufferer.

"I hope my mother didn't force you to come tonight," she said as they both turned their gazes away from the uncomfortable silent film.

He was so sick of this—everyone assuming he was nothing but a pawn to be pushed around by Chance women. "I'm a grown man. No one forces me to do anything." The words may have come out more stern than he meant them to, for she blinked and hunched her shoulders, as though warding off a blow.

"Right. It's just that my mother's new hobby is matchmaking. It's very embarrassing." And then she said, "I think I'll go get a devilled egg," and walked away.

A devilled egg? What the hell?

His mind was reeling. Had Lauren insinuated—no, practically told him—that Daphne was matchmaking, with him as Lauren's intended match? As Kirstin had pointed out, there weren't many unattached Chance girls left, and he barely knew Paisley. So, unless Daphne thought he'd come out of the closet and was jonesing for Josh, then it seemed Lauren was the one she had in mind for him.

The hope that he'd banished resolutely from his mind and heart began to flutter to life.

He went in search of her, thinking he'd first apologize for his abrupt words and then—what? Ask her to dinner? A movie? Marriage and three kids and a life on the farm?

As he walked toward where he'd last seen her, he got the opportunity to watch as a slick-looking guy said something to make her laugh. He had the dark good looks of an Italian movie star. All he needed was a few billion in the bank—and based on the clothes he was wearing, he probably had them—and he'd be the billionaire celebrity Kirstin had foreseen.

Cooper slapped him on the back. "Hey, Joe, how's it going?" Josh joined them, and Evan, who'd driven out for the party.

He hadn't seen Evan in a few years and he'd never seen a man look so happy. "Want to see my kid?" he said by way of greeting.

"Sure." Seemed like the right response.

"You'll be sorry," Cooper said, and snickered.

Joe hoped he wasn't going to be treated to a view of the birth and he half closed his eyes in case that was pushed in his face, but the photo Evan pulled up on his phone looked like an underwater geological survey. He had no idea if a joke was being played on him, so he looked up and raised his eyebrows.

"It's an ultrasound image," Evan said as though he saw those every day. "That's my kid in there."

"Where?"

Evan pointed to a blurry gray-black dot, shaped vaguely like a kidney bean. "Right there. It was so cool. At the ultrasound? We could hear its heartbeat."

"Congratulations."

"Thanks. I wish I could introduce you to my wife, but she stayed home. She's got a busy medical practice and she's hiring another doctor for when the baby comes."

Way too much information from a guy who'd once sent him sailing into a pond for singing a bad love song. At least Joe had never subjected another human being to pictures of the inside of a woman's uterus.

Cooper said, jutting his chin to where Lauren was still chatting with Romeo, "Think Matt's going to ditch Rose and run off with Lauren?"

Evan made a rude noise. "No. And if you weren't so immature you'd know it."

So, the Latin lover was Rose's fiancé. His evening just got better again. Cooper, never one to drop a subject that was annoying other people, said, "He wouldn't be the first. Remember the high school principal who was going to leave his wife for her? She was a high school senior."

Evan chuckled. "Mom and Dad almost home-schooled her, but luckily, the guy got transferred to another school. No, wait, remember the night we all went for pizza and when the waiter put Lauren's pizza in front of her and it was in the shape of a heart?" He shook his head. "Whoever made the pizza never even showed his face. He declared his love in pizza dough."

James joined them, having freed himself from Kirstin. "What are we talking about? Lauren's lovers? What about that guy who kept putting the same ad in the Missed Encounters section of the personals?"

Evan shook his head. "Or your friend who carved her in marble. Using his imagination, I hope." Then he threw back his head and laughed. "Or that kid who composed the worst love song ever and sang it outside Lauren's window?"

Silence.

He glanced around the group. "What?"

James and Cooper were both making awkward motions in his direction that Evan was not getting. Finally, feeling as though he were starring in a farce, Joe said, "That was me."

Evan looked stunned. "Really? Hey, I'm sorry. But you don't look a bit like that kid."

"Fourteen years ago, I was that kid."

"Well, better men than you have made that mistake. Don't worry about it."

And in that moment, the possibility that Lauren might actually like him popped like a soap bubble when you blow on it.

CHAPTER 14

Two weeks later

"**Y**ou're getting your makeup done professionally, with the rest of us, because I'm the bride," Rose looked like a scary boss bride, which she was. "And when I'm the bride, what I say goes."

Lauren knew her sister had a point, and how could she argue? How could she say to a woman who was supposed to be the focus of attention all day that when she, Lauren, put on makeup and looked her best, she'd overshadow her sisters?

Of course she couldn't say that. She'd sound vain and all about herself.

Why hadn't she had the courage to say no to being a bridesmaid? Maybe if she'd realized at the time that saying yes to one wedding meant being in a double header, she would have. But Rose and Marguerite? Who could have known?

Anyway, she loved her sisters. Of course she wanted to be a bridesmaid at their weddings. "You're right. I'm sorry. Count me in."

Marguerite, always more sensitive to people's feelings than

Rose, glanced between the two of them looking worried. "I don't mind. You're so beautiful anyway, you don't need makeup."

"Yes, she does," Rose retorted. "You know what she's like. If we don't drag her along to the salon, she'll do her hair herself in a single braid down her back and her entire makeup routine will be a swipe of ChapStick on her lips. I don't care if she's more beautiful than we are, it's our wedding, and Lauren's going to look like a bridesmaid."

There was no arguing with Rose when she made up her mind about something. Lauren understood that it was a mark of Rose's respect to want her to look her best.

So, she was the best sport she knew how to be, didn't say anything when a makeup artist named Louis gushed over her perfect skin, her beautiful eyes, and *oh my God the bone structure, the eyebrows, the lips.* Her hair was washed and curled and left to hang in ringlets down her back, and then she was creamed and painted and primped.

When Rose saw her, dressed in the pale pink dress they'd all agreed on, she said, "You look great, kid. And I'll know Matt really loves me if he doesn't beg you to run away with him."

Since Rose looked stunning in a slim-fitting designer wedding dress, and was one of the most confident women Lauren had ever known, she laughed at the joke, as she was meant to.

Marguerite wore a dress she'd sewn herself and it was just as perfect. More boho than designer, the lace was patterned with daisies. Marguerites, no doubt.

Lauren had been pondering the logistics and asked, "Is Dad giving both of you away?"

Marguerite said, "No. I asked Ben to give me away. He's the oldest boy, and besides, he's here so rarely I figured we'd have to guilt him into coming home."

Ben had some high-level hush-hush job in Washington, DC,

and rarely made it home. Lauren was impressed at Marguerite's ingenuity. "Nicely played, sis," she said.

There was a Greek Orthodox Church only twenty miles away, but since the girls weren't converting, they couldn't be married there. Rose admitted that Mrs. Vasilopolous had enacted a full Greek tragedy when she discovered the wedding would be officiated in the Chance family's garden by a nondenominational minister. A Vasilopolous uncle was giving a reading in Greek and the ceremony incorporated the wearing of floral crowns. Still, when she showed up the day before the wedding, she was dressed in heavy black more suitable for a funeral.

However, Paisley was keen to ask Alex and Matt's parents about some tricky aspects of Greek mythology and so they warmed up.

The day of the wedding dawned as sunny as though the Oracle of Delphi had predicted good fortune for the wedding couples. Alexei might be a champion food-truck chef, but he was no slouch with fine food, either. Under his direction, his staff had come up with a menu that catered to the traditional Greeks in the family, as well as offering the kinds of tiny things on silver trays that made Rose happy. Lauren had to hand it to Holly, who had somehow managed to combine the wishes of both sisters, and the Greek traditions, and made the wedding perfect for both.

She thought her bridesmaid's bouquet said it all. It was a mixture of daisies and wildflowers, which Marguerite loved, and three perfect blush roses, which typified the sister who'd been named for them. It shouldn't have worked, and yet it did.

As she walked down the grass aisle, Lauren felt swamped by love for all these people—her parents, her sisters and brothers, her new brothers-in-law, and especially the crew who had quietly rebuilt Jack's gazebo the night before. The women of the wedding party had all stayed in Portland at Rose's insistence, so they'd be able to have their hair and makeup done together. They'd laughed and cried a lot, and completely missed the work party at home rebuilding Jack Chance's gazebo. Well, not *re*building so much as *building* a sturdy structure that looked a lot like the one he'd found online.

Dad walked Rose up the aisle, looking so proud she wondered his shirt buttons didn't pop. Marguerite walked up the aisle on Ben's arm. Ben looked like a young Denzel Washington and he'd gained a sense of authority in his years working in DC. Not that he hadn't already had it; as the eldest of eleven kids, he was like a third parent.

Rose's voice wavered as she recited her vows, and that was enough to have Lauren sniffling and blinking back tears. The two grooms, both so dark and handsome, promised to love and cherish with such commitment that she believed she was witnessing two unions that would last forever. Marguerite's voice was barely audible, but no one had to hear her words. Her face said it all. She glowed with happiness.

Afterward, the party started. Kirstin said, "Is Ben single, do you know?"

"Actually, I don't. You'll never find anyone who guards his privacy better than Ben." She wondered if his upbringing had messed him up, but she honestly didn't think so.

Daphne had been pregnant with Ben by her professor at college, an African American who, married and with another family, wanted nothing to do with her or her baby. She'd met Jack on a Greyhound bus headed for Oregon and they'd married. The coolest thing about her parents was the way they'd collected kids over the years. Some were theirs by birth, and others were foster kids they'd come to love along the way. There was an iron-clad rule in their household: No one could know whether they were Jack and Daphne's natural born children or whether they'd been adopted, not until they were sixteen. Jack, who'd grown up in the foster care system, was determined that no child in his household would ever feel less important than another.

Truth was, by the time she'd reached sixteen, Lauren hadn't cared. She supposed, if she ever got around to having kids, that she'd want to know about genetics, but as far as she was concerned, Jack and Daphne were her parents. Ben was the only one of them who was obviously not the child of both Jack and Daphne, but he'd grown up well-adjusted and happy, though perhaps more secretive than the others. But then, he did something hush-hush for the government so even that was a plus.

While Lauren was standing there gazing at the gazebo that had been built in a latticework pattern, all painted in white, with candle holders hanging all ready to be lit when it got dark, James came up beside her. "What are you smirking at?" He followed her gaze. "I think we did a pretty good job. And I'll tell you one thing—it's for damned sure won't fall down. Or catch fire."

"I'm sure it won't. And we have Prescott the architect to thank for that."

"Are you kidding? You can thank Joe Benbow."

She turned to him in surprise. "Joe helped to build this thing?"

"Oh yeah. He came by last night to help. And being a fire-fighter, he is all about the safety of the structure. Honestly, he made Prescott look like a Saturday DIY carpenter."

She laughed at that. "Prescott is the ultimate perfectionist."

"I beg to differ. Joe Benbow is the ultimate perfectionist. Prescott is in distant second place. No kidding, if a giant meteor hits Oregon, that gazebo will still be standing. Ice ages will come and go, and that gazebo will still be standing. You're looking for a safe place in an earthquake? Throw yourself under that gazebo." She was still laughing when James wandered away to find Kimberly.

His place was soon taken by a man she'd never seen before. But he had an expression in his eyes that she recognized all too well. Her heart began to sink into her belly and as he looked at her, the way a man might who is dazzled by strong sunlight, she took an involuntary step backward.

"I'm George. One of Matt's friends. Well, colleagues, really. I'm a surgeon. Actually, a plastic surgeon. And I have to tell you that you are, without a doubt, the most perfect and beautiful woman I have ever seen. If everyone looked like you I'd be out of business."

She knew he meant well, but she was always uncomfortable when people commented on her looks. "Well," she said lightly, "you of all people know that beauty is only skin deep."

"No. Not yours. I can see that it goes all the way through. I didn't want to come to this wedding. I mean, Matt's a great guy and Rose is a friend, too, but I had to give up a sailing weekend. Now I know why I'm here. I was meant to meet you."

While he was talking, she had the opportunity to notice the wedding ring on his left hand. She said, somewhat tartly, "Is your wife here with you?"

He blinked as though he'd forgotten such a creature as his wife existed. He stared at her mouth as though he were planning to kiss her. "It was a mistake. I never should've married her. I knew in my heart I could do better. I'll talk to her tonight. I'll tell her that I've met the love of my life." He let out a humorless laugh. "It'll cost me, but it's worth it."

His wife would be well rid of him if *this* was his idea of how marriage worked, but she couldn't say anything, not if he was a friend of the groom. Besides, she felt a little bit guilty, as though by dressing up and looking her best, she was drawing trouble to her. It wasn't like she didn't have experience in situations exactly like this.

While she searched her mind for something to say and came up blank, she felt someone come up on her other side and slip an arm around her waist. Before she had a chance to register who it was, Joe said, "Hey, babe. I've been looking for you."

Then, when she turned toward him, she saw the understanding in his eyes.

Finally, she was safe.

He kissed her lightly on the lips and she nearly forgot that he had come to her rescue. She felt the impact of the mere brush of his lips all the way down to her toes.

The obnoxious plastic surgeon said, "Are you with him?" He sounded as though he couldn't believe she could be with anyone but him.

"Yes," she said. "Yes, I am." She'd never told a lie in her life that felt more true.

"Thanks for telling me." And then he turned tail and headed away. The minute he did so, Joe dropped his arm and took a step backward. "Hope I didn't intrude, but it looked to me like you needed rescuing."

"Oh, I did. Thank you." She thought for a moment. "He was so obnoxious, too. *And* he's married."

"Guy's an ass. I do feel kind of sorry for him, though. Seeing you for the first time, looking the way you do today?"

Joe was the only person she wanted to think she looked nice. She'd never fished for a compliment before, but she found herself doing so now. "You think I look nice?"

If she'd stuck him with a cattle prod he couldn't have jumped back further, or faster. "Sure I do. You're the best-looking friend I have. Definitely better looking than your brother James or the fire chief, Dan." She noted the way he emphasized the word *friend,* as though warning her they'd never be anything more.

She thought of the daisy she'd denuded of its petals and how its message had been that Joe did love her. She had to be brave. For once in her life, she had to tell a man how she felt.

What better place than this wedding, where she'd been treated to a display of the power of love? Several, actually. There were the brides and grooms, of course, but also Evan, being so careful with the newly pregnant Caitlyn, and her mom and dad, who acted as though every wedding was a renewal of their own vows. James and Kim, obviously taking notes for when it was their turn. With all these happy couples surrounding them, surely some of the magic would rub off?

But as she was about to speak, Alexei came up beside them. He said to Joe, "It's time."

Joe nodded and took a deep breath, then blew it out. "I haven't been this nervous going into a burning apartment complex," he said in a low voice.

What on earth?

Then, as she watched, Joe took off his jacket and hung it over a chair. One by one, a group of men headed for the gazebo. Her father lit the candles and seemed to turn on the magic. She watched both grooms, her brothers Ben, Evan, James, Josh, and Cooper, as well as a couple of Greek cousins she didn't know, climb up onto the stage along with Joe. All were down to shirt-sleeves.

Daphne walked by and said, "Oh, my. I think I need to sit down. I'm having a hot flash."

She thought maybe she was having some kind of flash herself as she watched so much male beauty collected in one place. Matt Vasilopolous took over the mic and said, "In Greece, we dance to celebrate a marriage. Mom and Dad, this is for you. Some of you may recognize the music from *Zorba the Greek.*"

And then he said some words in Greek, and a low, sultry beat began to play. Then an instrument she thought might be a zither. And she felt transported to the Greek isles as the group of men put their arms over each other's shoulders and began to dance.

She didn't even realize she was moving until she found herself closer to the stage. She wasn't the only one—all the women seemed drawn to watch. It was incredibly sexy watching these virile men dancing with a kind of deliberate joy. Her gaze was fixed on Joe, who fumbled a few times, but otherwise would have fit right in at a wedding in Athens. She and the other spectators began to clap in time to the music as the men kicked and jumped, and gyrated their hips.

"Oh, mercy," said a woman standing near her.

At the end of the dance, there was riotous applause, and Alex and Matt's parents ran up on the gazebo/stage to kiss both their boys. Maybe this dance made up for all the disappointment these two had suffered when both their boys married non-Greek women.

"Okay, everybody," Daphne yelled. "It's time for the brides to throw their bouquets. Come on, single girls, crowd around."

If there was ever a stupider, more old-fashioned tradition, Lauren didn't know what it was. In her opinion, throwing the bride's bouquet should be outlawed. She tried to hang back, but her friend Kirstin grabbed one of her hands and Paisley the other. They pulled her forward to the group of giggling women standing in a semicircle around the two brides who had taken over the gazebo. The rest of the wedding guests, the married women and all the men, gathered behind the singles.

"One at a time!" Daphne called.

"You go first," Marguerite said to her older sister. Rose didn't need to be persuaded. She checked out the group and then turned her back and threw her bouquet.

Clearly, she'd aimed for Kimberly, and her aim was true. Maybe she'd manipulated Fate a little, but when Lauren saw the way James's fiancée's eyes lit up and the way she held the bouquet against her chest, she forgave Rose for being high-handed.

Marguerite was next. She turned her back to the crowd, bent her knees, swung her arms, and launched her bouquet into the air.

Marguerite was a vegetable farmer, who dug and hoed and pulled weeds for a living. In her spare time, she practiced yoga. Her arms, therefore, were strong, and that bouquet sailed up high and over the group of single women, some of whom had their hands raised in an attempt to catch the flying flower missile. Once it had passed over her, Lauren was happy to watch the thing land, as long as it wasn't in her hands.

Suddenly, it lost velocity and came down—where it hit Joe on the shoulder and fell right into his arms.

The crowd broke up in laughter, and hooting, back-slapping, and joking. When he glanced up, she was surprised to see him looking right at her.

Then they both averted their gazes.

CHAPTER 15

*A*fter the brides and grooms had driven away—Marguerite and Alexei in her red truck, all washed and polished up for the occasion, and Rose and Matt in his fancymobile—the party continued without them.

Lauren kept hoping that Joe would come and find her, but he always seemed to be somewhere close enough that he could put an arm around her if she needed to ward off an overeager man, but otherwise laughing it up with her brothers, old friends, her folks... anyone, in fact, but her.

Around midnight he finally came up to her. The lights in the gazebo twinkled and romance was in the air like a sweet, elusive fragrance. Was he finally going to ask her to dance?

Instead, he said, "I had a great time tonight. You all did a fantastic job with the wedding."

Seriously? He was finally speaking to her and he wanted to discuss wedding planning? "Thanks. Mostly it was Holly and Mom who did the work."

He nodded, seeming to run out of wedding planning notes. Awkwardly, he held up the bouquet he'd ended up with. For a moment she thought he was going to present it to her.

"I'll take this home to my grandmother. I hope it will cheer her up. She's pretty sad that I'm leaving."

"You're leaving?" The words came out much louder and more harshly than she'd intended.

"Yeah. My boss called today. They can't give me any more time off. I can't blame the guy—he's been generous as it is."

Of course she could understand that. But wasn't there something between them? Did he angry-kiss every woman he dragged out of a burning building?

She didn't think so.

"I'll walk you to your car," she said, because who wouldn't want to prolong the most awkward conversation of her life?

"Okay." They walked out together. They must look a bit strange, with him carrying one of the bridal bouquets. Out in the big field where the cars were parked, it was quieter, but they could still hear the music.

She wouldn't get another opportunity to talk to him before he left. Here she was bursting with things she wanted to say to him, but didn't know how to begin.

Her sisters had been right when they'd teased her. She'd never been in a situation like this before. She had no practice at asking a man to be with her. All her experience had been in pushing them away.

How did she let him know she was interested without being too forward? She had no idea, so she went with, "I'll miss you." She stepped closer and tilted her face up, so he'd know she wanted him to kiss her. It left him room to avoid the kiss if he wanted to, and they could both pretend she wasn't throwing herself at him.

He stared at her lips for a moment and she felt warmth begin to spread. Then he shook his head, as though he had a sudden chill, and pulled her in for a hug.

A *hug*. He all but banged her on the back with his fist, like they were a couple of bros.

"I'll miss you, too." He stepped back. "I'll see you when I'm back next."

"When will that be?" She felt miserable and sad. Rejection sucked.

"My grandparents are probably putting their farm up for sale. I'll come back when it sells and help them move."

She couldn't believe what she was hearing. "Ernest and Velma are selling? But that farm is their whole life."

He pushed his toe into the ground. "I know, but they're getting older and having trouble finding good help. They're hoping to sell to a family who will keep running the farm. You know they'll pass your name on as the best vet around."

As though she were worried about losing business. She was worried about losing him! "When are you leaving?"

"Day after tomorrow. I've still got a few chores to do. You know Ernest—he likes to keep me busy."

"They'll miss you, Joe." What she meant was, *I'll miss you*, but she'd already told him that. He clearly didn't want her.

He stood there and she almost thought he was about to say something... And then he shook his head as though stopping himself. "Well, I'd better get going."

And he got into his SUV and drove away.

～

THE NEXT DAY dawned bright and all the Chance kids who were still in the area came by the family home. First, for the hearty breakfast and to congratulate Holly and Daphne on another fabulous wedding, and then to roll up their sleeves and get busy cleaning up the place.

They didn't need to take down the huge tent—the rental

people would do that—but they had to strip the linens from the tables, and put the glasses and plates and cutlery into the boxes they'd come in. There were ribbons and twinkle lights to put away and garbage to bag up.

"What do you want to do with the gazebo?" Ben asked his dad.

"Oh, leave it," Daphne said. "It's so pretty. We can put out a table and chairs and sit there in the summer."

"Besides," Jack said, "At the rate these kids are getting married, it's going to be in full-time use."

"You're right," James said. "In fact, Paisley said to me last night that one day she'd like to get married under that gazebo. It was a great idea, Dad."

Ben turned to Lauren. "How about you, sis? Do you want to get married here at home? Keep up the tradition?"

She had no idea why he was picking on her, but his words felt like worrying a fresh wound. "How am I ever going to get married, when the only man I care about is leaving town?"

The second the words were out, she regretted them. Only intense mental turmoil could have caused her to say aloud what she was thinking nonstop.

Immediately, all the well-meaning but nosy members of her family pounced.

"What do you mean?" Daphne put down a huge bowl of fruit salad as though she were in danger of dropping it. "He's leaving?"

"Who's leaving?" asked Prescott. "Is there something I'm supposed to know? How come I never know what's going on in my own family?"

Holly patted his knee. "Because you live in your own world, darling. You hardly ever see what's right under your nose."

Everyone else was staring at Lauren with looks ranging from

amusement to downright pity. Josh said, "So, beauty finally fell for a beast."

"Stop it. Joe Benbow isn't a beast," Daphne said. "He's a very nice young man. Although I will think he's a beast if he hurts my baby."

James snorted. "Joe Benbow is so much in love with Lauren that after they're together, I feel like I need to brush my teeth."

Everyone stared, but Josh, in a rare moment of twin understanding, nodded. "Like eating too much cotton candy. Totally get the same feeling from those two."

"They really are twins," Iris said. She was holding Liam, and Geoff was holding Mia. The two of them even swayed in unison.

"Then why is he leaving? If he's so crazy about me?"

"Have you given him any encouragement at all?" Ben asked her. "Guys like to know when a woman's interested in them. Otherwise, we worry that we'll make fools of ourselves."

"Of course I've given him encouragement." *Don't cry. Do not cry in front of everyone.* "But he moves away, or acts like he didn't notice."

"There was the angry kissing, though," Iris said. "He definitely noticed you then."

"Angry kissing?" Ben looked around. Naturally, all the women nodded, knowing what Iris was talking about, and all the men looked confused.

Quickly, Iris explained about the circumstances of the angry kissing.

"Yep," Ben said, nodding. "That confirms it. He wants you bad."

"Then why is he leaving?" Lauren wailed.

Josh said, "He did make a spectacular fool of himself over our Lauren. It's hard to come back from something like that."

"So how do I let him know that I want him?" Even saying the words made her feel hot and foolish.

Cooper had been thinking and suddenly he piped up. "I have an idea." And with a huge grin, he laid out his plan. "We don't have to return the sound system until tomorrow, right?"

THIS HAD to be the stupidest idea in the history of ideas.

If Lauren didn't come from a family of certifiable lunatics, she wouldn't currently be where she was, which was standing in the dark and cold outside Ernest and Velma's farmhouse.

In the background she could hear the sounds of a contented night. The cows were sleeping. The sky was clear, and all the lights in the farmhouse were out. In the dim light of the moon she could see that Joe had already packed his SUV. How many hours until he'd be on the road?

Would Cooper's crazy idea even work? But then, if it didn't, she'd be no worse off.

She was so tempted to leave, to get back into her truck and drive away as slowly and quietly as she'd arrived. No one would ever know. She could tell Cooper that his idea had been a failure. Who'd ever contradict her?

She would. She'd know that in the end she hadn't been brave enough to fight for the man she loved.

Love. Who'd have believed that she'd find it where she least expected to? In her own backyard.

Was there any hope at all for her? There was only one way to find out.

She got the items she needed out of the back of the truck—the guitar, mic, and amp—and set up as quietly as she could. She hadn't had time to write a song, so she'd gone with a karaoke favorite.

JOE COULDN'T SLEEP. Lying here in his old room, with his grandparents down the hall, all he could think of was that this might be the last time he slept here while they still owned the farm. Was he making a terrible mistake?

He lay on his back, his hands stacked under his head and wondered if he was a man who could only love once. He'd gone all in at the age of sixteen for a girl he could never have. In all the years since, he'd never come close to feeling the same way about someone else as he had about Lauren. Truth was, he still didn't.

It wasn't her looks. Sure, they'd drawn him to her initially, but it had been a long time since he'd been knocked over by her beauty. As he'd come to know her better, he'd seen beyond her looks to the woman she was inside. The one who loved animals, who tried never to hurt anyone's feelings—even the prize fools who fell at her feet.

They didn't see what was so great about her. Not the perfect looks, or stunning rack, but the woman who cared about all creatures great and small.

He knew now that he'd never find a woman whom he'd love as he loved Lauren. He sat bolt upright in bed. Had he really tried hard enough to let her know how he felt?

Of course he hadn't. He'd been going overboard trying to stay in the friend zone. Sure, he'd made a fool of himself once, but it hadn't killed him. What if he tried again? If he quit holding back and laid his heart on the line?

He'd go, tomorrow. He'd go to her before he left town and put his feelings out there for her. He'd make a fool of himself one last time.

Knowing he was going to go to Lauren, to see her again, if only to hear her tell him there was no more hope for him now than there had been fourteen years ago, made him feel better. He had a plan and at least he'd see her again.

As he was drifting off to sleep, he heard a strange sound, like the whine of a microphone that's too close to the amplifier. Like all farmers, he woke when any strange noise filtered through his consciousness. Was there something up with one of the animals?

As he had the thought, music blasted out suddenly into the night. Loud and jarring. What the hell?

Then he heard a voice, a voice he recognized even magnified through a mic. A voice he'd recognize anywhere on the planet— or in his dreams. "Joe Benbow, this song is for you."

He bolted out of bed and went to the window. Lauren had a guitar in her hand, which she played very badly, like she'd just learned two chords and had to concentrate to get them right. She sang into the mic. "And I-I-I-I-I... will always... love youuuu-uuu." The moonlight lit up her face, so very pretty, even as she pulled her eyebrows together in concentration, and opened her mouth wide, as though that might help her hit the notes.

It didn't.

For all her perfections, Lauren Chance wasn't much of a singer.

Lights went on down the hall and he heard Ernest say, "What on God's green earth is going on out there?"

A moment later, Grandma said quite sternly, "Turn the light out, Ernest, and be quiet."

Lauren went on singing, and playing, and a better man than he was would have run out there and stopped her and let this very interesting development go where it would. But he found he wasn't a better man. He was enjoying himself far too much.

He knew exactly how she felt—at least, he did if she was feeling the way he had all those years ago—the rush of hope, the fear of rejection, and the strange exhilaration of doing something so daring you were amazed you'd found the courage.

The song came to an end. She glanced up to his window and

he thought he'd remember her face for the rest of his life. The love shining out, the hope. The doubt. Did she sense him standing there, watching her?

She looked right at him and put the mic up to her mouth once more. "Joe, I came here to tell you that I'm in love with you and I don't want you to leave." She seemed to want to say more, but didn't know how. "I have office hours all day tomorrow if you want to come by. Okay, that's all." She put the mic down, then, almost as an afterthought, put it to her mouth again. "Sorry if I woke you, Ernest and Velma."

~

OH, she was going to make Cooper pay. Him and his stupid ideas. No doubt he'd snuck along behind her and filmed her complete humiliation so he could load it up on YouTube and laugh at her forever.

Not that it mattered anymore. She'd tried. She'd gone all the way. She'd made an absolute fool of herself in front of Joe, his grandparents, and a herd of cows. This was it. She was done.

At least, she thought as she picked up the guitar and mic, at least she'd put everything out there in the name of love. She'd been brave. As Paisley had quoted as she'd left the house, *"Better to have loved and lost than never to have loved at all."*

Though she wasn't so sure about that. Not when she had to live with this heavy feeling around her heart.

She crept toward her truck, though why she crept she didn't know, since they must all be awake by now. As she got nearer, she became aware of a solid, man-sized shape standing beside the driver's door.

Her heart began to pound. With hope, with dread. What if he wanted to tell her thanks but no thanks, as she'd said to him all those years ago?

When she was within speaking distance, he said, "You are a terrible singer."

"I know."

He took the mic and guitar from her and loaded them into the truck bed for her, like he was the hotel valet service. Her heart was still pounding and she still didn't know what he was thinking. Except that she shouldn't give up her day job.

Then he turned and stepped closer. And in the moonlight, she saw everything she needed to see. "Did you really mean that?" he asked softly.

"You think I'd make a fool of myself like this if I didn't mean it? I don't think I can ever come here again. Poor Ernest and Velma. They'll probably demand a new vet."

"I don't think so. I think they love you."

Well, that was something. "Do they?"

"Yep. But not as much as I do."

"Really?"

"Are you kidding? I've been in love with you half my life. I just never thought I had any hope."

"Oh, Joe." This time, when she lifted her face in mute invitation, he took full advantage, pulling her slowly into his arms and kissing her until she thought she'd faint from delirium and lack of breath.

She wrapped her arms around him, and he wrapped his around her. "You know, I won't always look like this."

He chuckled. "I don't care. I don't love your face, though it's pretty. I love the woman you've grown into. The one who risks her life for a bunch of chickens."

She tilted her face up. "I thought you were angry with me for that."

"I am. And don't you ever do it again."

"I can't guarantee that."

He smiled, as if he'd expected that. "I love that you care about animals, and never want to hurt anyone's feelings."

"I was thinking, that when you go back, maybe I could come visit you on some of my weekends off? And maybe you'd come here for some of your time off?"

He squeezed her so hard she thought a rib might crack. "What if I moved here? Permanently?"

She couldn't believe what she was hearing. "That would be the best news I could imagine."

He told her that James had offered him a job, and that he hated the idea of Ernest and Velma selling. "Would you ever be happy living on a farm in Hidden Falls?"

"Oh, Joe. I would be so happy I'd feel like I needed to pinch myself every morning to make sure I was awake."

"Oh, you're awake," he said, and then his mouth came down over hers. When he raised his head again, his eyes glinted. "Or we're both dreaming."

When he kissed her again she knew that all her dreams had come true.

I hope you enjoyed *The Daisy Game*. I'd be thrilled if you'd leave a review. I have more books planned for *The Chance Series*. Best way to be notified when a new book releases is to sign up for my newsletter at NancyWarrenAuthor.com

A Note from Nancy

Dear Reader,

Thank you for reading my *Take a Chance* series.

I hope you'll consider leaving a review and please tell your friends who like contemporary romance and family sagas.

Review wherever you purchased *The Daisy Game* or on Goodreads or BookBub.

Join my newsletter for a free prequel, *Tangles and Treasons*, the exciting tale of how the gorgeous Rafe Crosyer was turned into a vampire.

I hope to see you in my private Facebook Group. It's a lot of fun. www.facebook.com/groups/NancyWarrenKnitwits

Until next time,
Happy Reading,

Nancy

Nancy writes heartwarming, humorous romances and quirky cozy mysteries. The best way to keep up with new releases, plus enjoy bonus content and prizes is to join Nancy's newsletter at NancyWarrenAuthor.com or join her in her private Facebook group www.facebook.com/groups/NancyWarrenKnitwits

∾

Take a Chance series

Meet the Chance family, a cobbled together family of eleven kids who are all grown up and finding their ways in life and love.

Chance Encounter - Prequel

Kiss a Girl in the Rain - Book 1

Iris in Bloom - Book 2

Blueprint for a Kiss - Book 3

Every Rose - Book 4

Love to Go - Book 5

The Sheriff's Sweet Surrender - Book 6

The Daisy Game - Book 7

Take a Chance Box Set - Prequel and Books 1-3

The Almost Wives Club

An enchanted wedding dress is a matchmaker in this series of romantic comedies where five runaway brides find out who the best men really are!

The Almost Wives Club: Kate - Book 1

Second Hand Bride - Book 2

Bridesmaid for Hire - Book 3

The Wedding Flight - Book 4

If the Dress Fits - Book 5

The Almost Wives Club Box Set - Books 1-5

Vampire Book Club: A Paranormal Women's Fiction Cozy Mystery

Crossing the Lines - Prequel

The Vampire Book Club - Book 1

Chapter and Curse - Book 2

A Spelling Mistake - Book 3

Vampire Knitting Club: Paranormal Cozy Mystery

Tangles and Treasons - a free prequel for Nancy's newsletter subscribers

The Vampire Knitting Club - Book 1

Stitches and Witches - Book 2

Crochet and Cauldrons - Book 3

Stockings and Spells - Book 4

Purls and Potions - Book 5

Fair Isle and Fortunes - Book 6

Lace and Lies - Book 7

Bobbles and Broomsticks - Book 8

Popcorn and Poltergeists - Book 9

Garters and Gargoyles - Book 10

Diamonds and Daggers - Book 11

Herringbones and Hexes - Book 12

Ribbing and Runes - Book 13

Cat's Paws and Curses - A Holiday Whodunnit

Vampire Knitting Club Boxed Set: Books 1-3

Vampire Knitting Club Boxed Set: Books 4-6

The Great Witches Baking Show

The Great Witches Baking Show - Book 1

Baker's Coven - Book 2

A Rolling Scone - Book 3

A Bundt Instrument - Book 4

Blood, Sweat and Tiers - Book 5

Crumbs and Misdemeanors - Book 6

A Cream of Passion - Book 7

Gingerdead House - A Holiday Whodunnit

The Great Witches Baking Show Boxed Set: Books 1-3

Abigail Dixon 1920s Mysteries

Death of a Flapper - Book 1

Toni Diamond Mysteries

Toni is a successful saleswoman for Lady Bianca Cosmetics in this series of humorous cozy mysteries.

Frosted Shadow - Book 1

Ultimate Concealer - Book 2

Midnight Shimmer - Book 3

A Diamond Choker For Christmas - A Holiday Whodunnit

For a complete list of books, check out Nancy's website at NancyWarrenAuthor.com

ABOUT THE AUTHOR

Nancy Warren is the USA Today Bestselling author of more than 90 novels. She's originally from Vancouver, Canada, though she tends to wander and has lived in England, Italy and California at various times. While living in Oxford she dreamed up The Vampire Knitting Club. Favorite moments include being the answer to a crossword puzzle clue in Canada's National Post newspaper, being featured on the front page of the New York Times when her book Speed Dating launched Harlequin's NASCAR series, and being nominated three times for Romance Writers of America's RITA award. She has an MA in Creative Writing from Bath Spa University. She's an avid hiker, loves chocolate and most of all, loves to hear from readers! The best way to stay in touch is to sign up for Nancy's newsletter at NancyWarrenAuthor.com or www.facebook.com/groups/Nancy-WarrenKnitwits

To learn more about Nancy and her books
NancyWarrenAuthor.com